SUMMER LOVIN' AT CLOUD LAKE

ANNIE LYNN MARENE

Copyright © 2022 by Tenderholt Creative

All rights reserved.

No part of this book may be reproduced in any form or by any electronic or mechanical means, including information storage and retrieval systems, without written permission from the author, except for the use of brief quotations in a book review.

CHAPTER 1

Madison watched the steam rise from the dark liquid as she poured coffee into a worn white mug. She already had two sugars, one creamer, and a spoon ready to go. She wondered how many cups of coffee she must have poured in her lifetime. Probably millions over her twenty-six years and most of them right here in the café. Moving closer to the window, she gazed past red gingham curtains towards the quiet sunlit shore of the lake. The bright sunbeams held the promise of another beautiful summer day.

The first sip of coffee always tasted like magic. It cleared the dusty old cobwebs out of her mind so she could wake up and get to work. Her golden bangs weren't long enough to stay in her messy bun, and she absently brushed them off to one side. Her blue eyes brightened as she glanced around the dining room.

A row of vinyl booths gleamed from a good scrubbing. Oak tables and chairs lined up in a tidy row. The staff had dusted the blinds under the curtains and hung them low enough to keep out some of the morning glare from the sun. They had swept and mopped the tiled floors until they sparkled. Everything in the dining room looked polished, clean, and in order. Her heart filled with pride as she inspected the Sunflower Café. Her staff had done another excellent job of getting things clean and ready for the day.

Her mornings were routine. Madison arrived first, to unlock the employee entrance. Her next order of business was always to start the coffeepots. Methodically, she would walk through the restaurant, turning on lights and making sure everything was clean, stocked and ready to go. A well-prepared restaurant helped ensure that shifts went smoothly.

After she inspected everything, she headed to her office to grind through paperwork. She had graduated from college with a degree in business management, but this part of running the café frustrated her. Madison worked on the paperwork first to get it out of the way. She would never understand how her father did it all before computers came along.

Settled into the well-worn office chair, Madison chewed at her bottom lip and turned on the computer. When her father ran the restaurant, he had the desk pushed against the back wall of the office. Madison took over and moved it to the middle of the office. It made the office a tight fit, but she liked to have the office door in front of her. The rest of the café – from the chrome napkin holders to the neon open sign to their recipe for pancakes – remained unchanged.

Madison struggled to concentrate on her work. She listened to the back door open and close as the cooks, dishwashers, and servers made their way in for their shifts. The staff appeared to be in a good mood. They laughed and chatted while they finished getting the restaurant ready. Madison hired her staff carefully, and it paid off. It might be just a country café, but her employees were excellent workers.

Her phone rang, breaking her out of her musings. Her realtor's name flashed across the screen. Madison froze for a moment and wondered if something had gone wrong. She picked up the phone.

"Hello?"

"Madison. Good morning. I hope I'm not disturbing you this early, but I know you get busy."

"It's great that you called early. We don't open for another fifteen minutes. Is everything okay?" Madison toyed with a rip in the vinyl arm of her chair.

"Everything is fine. I wanted to be sure you had your appointment with the bank all set. I would hate to see someone else buy up the resort when you're so close to owning it."

"Is someone else interested?" Madison hadn't heard of anyone else expressing interest. She gripped the armrest and sat up straighter.

"I... I'm not sure. I've heard a rumor and I haven't been able to touch base with the Davises."

"They have a lot of family in for their anniversary. Maybe they're just busy."

"You're probably right. Still, let's keep pushing forward. The deal isn't over until everyone's signed off on it."

"You'll call me if you hear anything?" Madison bit at her lip again.

"Definitely. Have a good day. We'll talk soon."

An extremely blonde head with its short hair spiked high popped into the office doorway. It was Chloe, her bright brown eyes shining and alert. She carried a coffeepot in one hand and a mug in the other. "Morning Madison. Need a refill?"

"Sure, come on in." Madison smiled at her. "How's it going out there?"

"It's all sunshine and rainbows!" Chloe said. She filled their mugs with fresh coffee and set the pot on the corner of the desk before settling into the chair. She wrapped her hands around her cup of coffee. "How is it going in here?"

"Good enough, but I can't wait for you to start running the café."

"Are you sure about this? I can stick to looking pretty, delivering fried eggs and toast, and refilling coffee cups out front."

"You will be wonderful. You know what you are doing. The staff listens to you. You understand the paperwork, even the financials. But I'm not surprised at that part. I've seen how fast you are at calculating your tips." Madison couldn't resist teasing Chloe. "Seriously, you'll be a skilled manager."

"I am pretty fabulous!" Chloe struck a dramatic pose and fluttered her thick eyelashes. "But enough about me. How are your grand designs going? Are you ready to take over the world?"

Madison tried to smile enthusiastically. "I'm not sure about the entire world, but yes, I'm ready. I meet with the banker tomorrow to complete the financial paperwork and the realtor Friday to complete the purchase paperwork. If all goes well, I'll own the Cloud Lake Resort by next week."

"Then why do you look nervous?"

"I just had a call from the realtor. There may be someone else interested in the property."

"No way! After all this time? Wouldn't someone have said something? We're the gossip hub of Cloud Lake."

Madison laughed. "You're right. It's probably nothing. Everything is going according to plan."

"Our very own business tycoon. Someday you'll own the entire lake."

"No way!" Madison laughed. "I'm not greedy and I love our community just the way it is. It's strange how the resort has been off the market for months, though. I don't understand. It seems to make money. I thought for sure someone would buy it before I gathered the funds."

"You've got it all under control, thank goodness. And it would have been awful if Andy and Molly had shut down the resort so they could retire. They deserve to spend time with their kids and grandkids, but who knows what someone else would do with the place."

"They will spend time with their kids this week. They're all staying in the cabins so Andy and Molly can enjoy the week off before their fiftieth anniversary party on Saturday. Their family is renting cabins all over the place." Madison glanced at the clock and stood, forgetting about the last of her coffee.

Chloe kept talking to her. "We have a few minutes. Finish your coffee while it's warm. I want to ask you about Thursday, anyway."

Madison stayed standing but picked up her mug. She eyed the clock again. "Why, what's happening on Thursday?"

"We're all going tubing! You'll come with, won't you? It's going to be so fun."

Tubing. Madison tried not to grimace. She knew tubing would be fun, but it meant an afternoon away from work. Summer season kept her busy. She wanted to hire more staff for the café and had interviews set up all week. There were a few last tasks to get done to purchase the resort. After signing off on the paperwork, she would need to hire staff to help her run the resort. Tearing herself away to float down the river on an inner tube, slathered in sunscreen and drinking seltzers, wasn't on her list of priorities. But it sounded good. Excellent, in fact. And it had been a while since she'd spent time together with her friends.

"Aren't we getting a little old for tubing?" Madison eyed Chloe with suspicion.

"No way. I went a few weeks ago with my boyfriend. It's pretty tame on the weekdays, but still a lot of fun."

Chloe saw the hesitation on Madison's face but kept at it. "I know you usually take Wednesdays off, but Tonya said she'd switch days so you can go. Her son and his family are coming in Wednesday, and she'd rather have it off to get them settled in." Chloe looked at her expectantly.

"And she doesn't want her Thursday off to be with them?"

Chloe shook her head. "Nope, they'll be spending time at their in-laws, too. Sounds like they are trying to pack a lot of visiting into a few short days."

Madison sighed. "You knew that would talk me into it. All right. You win. I shouldn't, but maybe a day full of sunshine is just what I need. And maybe I'll float into tall, tan, and handsome while we're out there."

Madison and Chloe walked out of the office into the kitchen.

"Maybe he'll have a twin!"

"I'm a twin."

Madison and Chloe glanced over at the grill. The look of innocence on Benny's face didn't fool anyone.

"Benny, you have four older sisters and no brothers. Since when are you a twin?" Madison knew her staff.

"Astrologically I am. I'm a Gemini! Get it?" He wiggled his dark eyebrows and twitched his thick mustache at them.

"Oh Benny, that one was corny," Chloe said.

Madison groaned and switched the subject. "Your nephew, Landon, is coming in for an interview today. Which sister does he belong to?"

"Shawna, the second oldest. He's such a great kid. You're going to love him. His sense of humor takes the cake."

Chloe couldn't stop herself and blurted out, "Oh no."

"Oh yes. He's a chip off his old uncle. For sure." He peered at Madison. "You're going to hire him, right?"

"I hope so. He interviewed well over the phone, and we could use another dishwasher."

"He'll be great. Hey, did you hear about the space restaurant?"

Madison and Chloe shook their heads no.

"It had great food, but no atmosphere."

"Benny, Benny, Benny. Your jokes are terrible!" Chloe groaned.

"You laughed at them all in high school, Chloe." Benny winked at her.

"Seriously, we were kids."

"You two are still kids. And all of us have to get to work. I need to unlock the doors. Are you about ready, Benny?" Madison asked.

"Yes, ma'am." Benny saluted her. "Did you hear the rumor about the butter?"

Madison knew he wouldn't give up. "No, what about the butter?"

"Well, if you don't know, I'm not going to spread that one."

Madison and Chloe gave in. They shook their heads and laughed together as they made their way to the front. Madison knew she would miss these moments. She'd still be around to oversee the restaurant. She had to ensure it continued to run smoothly, but it wouldn't be the same. Even though people seemed to come and go, her employees still felt like family. The restaurant had always been a big part of her life.

And yet, another part of her needed a change, and it wouldn't quiet down. She needed a new challenge and wanted to do something closer to her degree. She intended to take the quaint resort and transform it. Madison loved a project with endless possibilities and this piece of the lake held potential. As an event center, it would be a wonderful place to hold weddings, reunions, or retreats. She could spend the whole day planning and dreaming, but she saw a small crowd of people gathering around the café doors.

Madison pulled the waitstaff together for a quick huddle. She went over the morning information, gave them a pep talk and let them know her door was always open if they needed anything. The staff left the huddle full of smiles and ready for their customers.

The day had barely begun, but it started off right. Madison had a feeling the entire day would follow suit. She looked forward to one of those days where steps were a little lighter and smiles a little brighter. If she could capture the good vibes in a bottle, she would. Instead, she went with it. She enjoyed the good times while they lasted. Life could be difficult, and Madison learned to appreciate a good day even more.

She walked over to the front door. The customers were already chatting together about the morning catch of fish and how beautiful the sun was as it rose over the lake. She unlocked the door and greeted them all with a cheerful "Good morning, everybody."

CHAPTER 2

Madison loved the morning crowd. She stood by the door and welcomed them as they came in. She didn't even have to seat most of them. The regular customers had their spots and went to them on their own. They either sat at the counter by the wait station, or the tables closest to it. Madison wondered the reason for it. Did they pick their seats so they could chat amongst themselves, or was it to sit closest to the hot coffee for their refills?

"Now just a minute, Gladys, you can't bring Jameson in here. He'll have to wait out in the car."

"Oh, come now Madison. He's so small and he'll stay right in my purse and he's a very good dog."

Madison knew Gladys meant well, but she also knew Jameson. The half teacup poodle, half Chihuahua terrorized everyone. "Nope. No dogs allowed. What if the health inspector saw him? I'd be put out of business." She wasn't sure if they would actually shut her down, but she wasn't about to find out.

Gladys argued another minute for the sake of arguing before relenting and putting Jameson out in the car. She fussed and sniffed even though she left the car running for him and had a temperature sensor to monitor how warm it was in the car. She took good care of him even if she overindulged him sometimes.

"One crisis averted," Madison mumbled to herself. "I wonder what else the day will bring."

"What was that?" Mr. Olson peeked over his reading glasses at her.

"I was talking to myself, Mr. Olson. How are you doing today?"

"I'm right as rain and we could sure use some around here. Wouldn't want the lakes to all dry up on us, now would we."

"No, we sure don't, Mr. Olson. That would be a real travesty." She hoped her eyes didn't betray her inner laughter.

"It sure would. You've got that right." He nodded enthusiastically.

"Where's the rest of your crew today?"

"They all abandoned me." Mr. Olson explained that Floyd had to drive to another city to see a doctor. Edward was feeling under the weather and wanted to stay home to rest. Max was visiting his son in Colorado because his grandson was getting married.

"That's nice. Weddings are always an enjoyable time."

"He says it was a real nice place. Much nicer than the service hall in town."

Madison smiled. That's exactly why she wanted to buy the resort. It had an empty grassy area big enough for a large building. She would transform the resort into a magical place for weddings and gatherings. She couldn't wait to usher joyful couples into their new lives of wedded bliss in a setting that was beautiful and romantic.

In the meantime, Madison needed another cup of coffee herself. She had no idea where she'd left her old cup. She always got busy or distracted and left them everywhere. It wasn't that she was absent minded. Her mind simply held on to more important things and forgot about coffee mugs. She took a new one off the shelf and prepared her cup just the way she liked it.

"Are you going to share that coffee around?" Dylan, one of the construction workers at the counter, held up his coffee cup. Madison loved Dylan's deep, gravelly voice. She had quite the crush on him in high school, but he never noticed her back then. It didn't surprise her. A senior and a freshman felt like a big difference in high school. And he had chased after his crush, Amy. He had talked her into marrying him. Now, their baby, Daniel James or D.J. for short, made three.

"Didn't Chloe fill your cup a moment ago?"

"I had a late night and D.J. doesn't sleep. I need all the caffeine I can get."

"Some days are tough." Madison filled his cup and topped off the rest of the cups on the counter.

She glanced over at the Donaldsons to see how they were doing. Of all the regulars, they needed the least amount of attention. They would each order a bowl of oatmeal with raisins. When they finished, they would each have one cup of hot tea, no refills. He would read the paper for about an hour, and she would read Agatha Christie novels while she waited for him. They never said much and kept to themselves off to the side. Madison was about to check on them, but a group of ten people came spilling through the door.

They were in their early twenties and looked like they hadn't gone to bed yet. These sorts of groups sometimes came in on the weekends, but it was only Tuesday. Madison grabbed a handful of menus.

"Good morning. Are tables okay?"

"Yeah, sure." The guy who spoke looked like he had slept on the forest floor. He wore a torn shirt, mud-streaked shorts, and he had a twig sticking out of his hair.

"Come on. Let's get some coffee and food into you."

A girl wearing sunglasses and a pink shirt with Hot Girl printed across the chest spoke up. "No way. No coffee. I need soda. I need water. I need biscuits and gravy."

"We can handle that." Madison got them to their tables in the side section. She had no intention of handing the group off to an employee. The staff could handle the regulars and she'd keep the trouble to a minimum with this group. She took their drink orders and headed over to the wait station.

"I made a tray of waters. I can deliver it while you get their drinks ready."

"Thanks Chloe. I appreciate it." Madison quickly filled their drink orders. She was afraid if she gave them her little cow cream pitchers, they would walk off with them. Instead, she piled the little plastic individual servings into a bowl for them to use. Carefully, she checked over the tray to make sure she didn't forget anything.

Chloe laughed when she came back behind the counter. "One of them says he is in love with me. He keeps saying it's love at first sight. Another one said the first guy was a liar and asked for my phone number. The girl sitting next to him said to forget both of them – they were broke losers, and she had to pay for their breakfast."

"Wonderful. Were we ever that young?" Madison grinned at her friend.

"Yes, like 5 years ago. We're not that old!"

Madison didn't bother responding. It had been a long time since she felt young and carefree. She tried to keep herself from sighing as she dropped off the drinks and took their orders. She waited patiently while it took them several minutes to figure out what they wanted. They decided on their orders, including the girl who still wanted biscuits and gravy. Madison hurried to get everything entered.

"You ought to charge those kids double."

"I ought to charge you double, Mr. Trouble." Madison sassed right back. When Mr. Bunting had first visited the restaurant, she couldn't connect with him. He had been a lawyer and mayor in a town about an hour away. When he retired, he found himself a place on the lake and began teaching himself to cook. His plan had not gone well. He often came in for breakfast to avoid his own rubbery eggs and burnt toast.

In the beginning, the staff thought he was quiet and grumpy. After a while, Madison teased him about being such a grouch in the mornings and he started teasing her back. Now he dished it out before she even had a chance to say hi.

Madison glanced over at him. "How are your eggs today?"

"Just terrible. I ought to complain to the owner."

"Ha! And let me guess. Your tip was about charging those kids double."

"You win the grand prize of... nothing."

Madison knew better. For an old grouch, he tipped generously.

Benny didn't take long to whip up orders. Chloe helped Madison deliver the food to her tables. Everything seemed relatively quiet. Madison quit tensing her shoulders and took a deep breath.

She snuck back to her office to prepare for her morning interviews. She found the paperwork she needed and placed everything on clipboards. Madison brought it all out to the host stand.

An explosion of laughter erupted from her tables. She grabbed a pot of coffee on the pretense of giving them refills and went to check on them. When she arrived at the table, the girl in the pink t-shirt lay with her face in her biscuits and gravy.

"Oh, my goodness! Is she all right? What happened?"

Her friends laughed. The guy with the twig in his hair spoke up. "She's okay. She always falls asleep on us."

This started the group laughing again. The noise of it woke the girl up. She sat up with a snort and stared at her plate. "Hey, there's a hair in my biscuits and gravy!"

Madison's eyes were wide. "Yes, and there is gravy all over your face! You fell asleep on your plate!"

The table of friends stared at the girl.

"Again?" she asked.

They erupted into another round of laughter.

Chloe came over to check out the commotion. "What in the world?"

Madison asked Chloe to get the girl a fresh order of food. The group asked for it to go. They wanted to get back to the campground to sleep it off. Madison told Chloe to add some bottled water for the gravy-faced girl. She was going to need it.

"Thanks for coming in today." Madison tried to look stern as she addressed the table. "I want you all to take care of each other though, okay? Make sure this girl drinks some water and doesn't get overheated while she's sleeping. Do you have a sober driver?"

One of the girls explained she and her boyfriend arrived that morning and would drive everyone back safely.

"Outstanding. Anything else I can help you all with?"

The guy with the twig stood and rubbed his stomach. "Nope. This place is great. See you next time!"

With that, the table left the café. Madison checked her watch. It read 9:30. She wondered how the rest of her day would go.

The first interview walked in promptly at 10:00. It should have been a nice first impression, but she wore flip-flops, cut-off shorts and a loose tank over a bikini top. Madison didn't think it would go well, but she greeted the girl with a warm smile.

"Good morning. You must be Kendra. I'm Madison."

"Sure, we did the phone interview thing."

"Yes, we did. Would you like something to drink while we talk?"

"Uh, sure. I'll have a lemonade."

Madison called over to Chloe, "Will you bring us a couple of lemonades?"

"Coming right up."

Madison led the way to a booth off to the side.

"So, Kendra, how are you today?"

"I'm good."

Madison waited a beat before moving on. "Can you tell me a little about yourself?"

"Uhm, I'll be a senior at Forrest County High."

Again, Madison waited a moment to see if the girl had anything more to say. Chloe dropped off the lemonades. "This is Chloe.

She'll be promoted to manager in a month or so. Chloe, this is Kendra."

"Hi." Kendra wasn't much of a talker.

Chloe tried to get something out of her. "It's great to meet you. Are you having a pleasant summer?"

"Yeah, sure."

Madison glanced at Chloe and wrote 110 on the interview sheet.

Chloe nodded and said, "Well, I better get back to work. Have a good day."

The poor girl said nothing. She didn't say much for the rest of the interview, either. She drank her lemonade and gave one-word or two-word answers to every question. Madison gave up and cut the girl loose. Kendra made a beeline for the door and Madison went back to the wait station.

"What did you tell her?" Chloe asked.

"I told her I had a few more interviews and I would call her by the weekend."

"Even with the 110?"

Rachel, one of the younger servers, was standing near them. She asked, "What's a 110?"

Chloe smiled wryly and surveyed the ground.

Madison explained, "It means I'm not interested. It's a way for me to mark the paper no without saying no. That way if I have a lot of interviews or get busy, it's already written down."

"I don't get it." Rachel continued, "Why 110 though?"

"Here, I'll show you." Madison took out a pen and made a slash between the ones. 110 turned into N o.

"Oh, my gosh, it literally makes a NO. That's so cool. But kind of sad. But cool."

"It's my little secret. Don't go spreading it around." Madison winked at Rachel.

"I won't. Your secret is safe with me." Rachel glanced around as if checking to make sure no one else could listen in. She decided it was safe to talk and continued. "I'm surprised you even interviewed Kendra."

"Why is that?" Chloe asked.

"She hardly ever talks. She gets good grades and everything, but the teachers never call on her because she barely answers."

"Her phone interview went well. I thought she would be a good fit."

Rachel giggled. "It probably wasn't even her. She probably had her older sister or one of her friends pretend to be her."

Madison sighed. "That would explain it. That's too bad. We could use another waitress. All right ladies, we better get back to work."

CHAPTER 3

*I*nstead of finding some work to do, Madison slipped into the kitchen. "Hey Benny."

"You forgot to have breakfast again, didn't you?"

"Yes, and my stomach is growling."

"Do you want a Big Benny or a Little Benny?"

"Just a little. It's getting close to lunch, and I have your nephew's interview in a few minutes."

Benny took a tortilla out of his private stash and added some fries, an egg, cheese, and a slice of bacon. He handed her a bottle of hot sauce with the plate. They didn't have anything with tortillas on the menu, but the kitchen staff always seemed to bring them in. They made burritos out of everything and anything.

Madison brought her breakfast taco into her office, doused it in hot sauce, and took a bite. She thought about adding the Big Benny and Little Benny to the menu. She made a note to have Chloe check on the costs and decide if they should order them.

Most of her morning crowd stuck with bacon and eggs, pancakes, or their famous cinnamon rolls, but maybe she could offer them on the weekends.

Her to-do list grew faster than she could check items off, and she worked nonstop. Overwhelmed, Madison leaned back in her chair and stared at the ceiling, trying to destress for a minute.

"Madison?" Rachel stood in the office doorway.

"What's up?" Madison straightened up in her seat.

"Benny's nephew, I mean Landon, is here."

"I'll be out in a minute."

Madison stretched in her chair. She took a picture off the desk. Her dad stood at the grill holding a spatula. He wore a white apron and had a huge grin on his face. Her mom smiled as she reached up top for an order. She wore the gold waitress dress they used for a uniform when they opened the café. They made it seem effortless. With care, she set the frame back on her desk.

Letting go of the café was bittersweet. The excitement and challenge of buying the resort and transforming it appealed to Madison but leaving the restaurant and its memories behind proved to be harder than she expected. Finding her own path and following her own dreams felt like losing her parents all over again. Her thoughts were heavy, but she put on a smile and went out to meet Landon.

"Good morning, Landon. I'm Madison."

"Hello Madison." Landon reached out to shake her hand. He must have forgotten he still held his phone in his hand. He tripped a little as he moved forward and launched it into her chest.

"Ouch! Wow that smarts."

Landon stood there, looking stunned.

"Landon? Are you all right?" Madison asked.

He tried to answer and squeaked. He coughed and tried again. "Yes ma'am. I'm okay. Are you okay?"

"I'll be fine. Don't worry about it. Let's start over." Madison held out her hand for him to shake. He took it and pumped it up and down vigorously.

"Would you like something to drink while we interview?"

"No ma'am. I'm fine. Thanks."

"Just call me Madison, all right?"

"All right." Landon grinned at her. "Madison."

She grabbed a clipboard and led the way to the same booth where she had sat with Kendra. They were almost there when Landon tripped over his feet again. He ran into Madison, who, in turn, slammed into the booth. Madison righted herself and peered at his shoes.

"Ma'am. Madison. I'm so sorry. I... what are you looking at? Are you okay?"

"I just wanted to see if your shoelaces were tied."

"Oh right. Yep, they're tied. Maybe I should go. I should go." Landon babbled.

"No, it's really all right. Let's take a seat."

They slid into a booth. Chloe came over with a cup of coffee for Madison.

"Landon, this is Chloe. She's going to be manager here in a few months."

"Nice to meet you, Chloe." Landon managed to shake Chloe's hand without incident.

"It's nice to meet you too, Landon. Enjoy your interview."

"Yes ma'am. I mean Chloe."

Chloe winked at him before she walked away. Landon blushed beet red. Madison ignored his embarrassment and moved on.

"So, Landon, why do you want to work at the Sunflower Café?"

"I want to make money."

Madison smiled at his honesty.

"I mean, Benny says this place is great. He loves working here. I thought I would like it here too."

"That's great Landon. We love having Benny work here."

Landon seemed to relax, and the rest of the interview went easier. Madison wondered if he would work out. She'd have to check his reference. He seemed young, but he had mowed lawns for one of the local lawn care companies the summer before. Hopefully Benny wouldn't give her too much trouble about taking her time to hire him.

Madison slid out of the booth. "Thanks for coming in today. I'll get back to you after I check your reference."

"Okay, have a good day." Landon made his way to the door. Instead of pulling it open, he tried to push the door and landed face first in the glass. He turned and saw everyone staring at him. He gave a funny little wave, yanked the door open, and ran out to his car.

Chloe spoke first. "He sure is an interesting young man."

"Ah, yes. Very polite though."

"Yes ma'am! Very polite." Chloe grinned at Madison.

"Don't you dare start ma'am-ing me!"

"Well, what did you think of him?"

"I think I should have you take over the interviews. It's so hard for me to let go around here."

Chloe shrugged. "I'm ready when you are. Are you avoiding the question?"

"Maybe. I'm nervous about him being around our dishes. Clumsy and dishware don't mix." Madison took her turn to shrug. "I'll talk to Benny and try to figure it out."

"Talk to me about what? Are you going to hire Landon?" Benny came up to fill his coffee mug.

"Is he always so clumsy?"

"What happened?"

Madison gave him a quick replay of the interview. "I'm a little worried about our dishes, Benny."

"Naw, he was just nervous. Maybe he's still getting used to his last growth spurt. My sister said his new shoes are two sizes bigger than the last ones. He's a good kid. I promise. He'll be fine."

"I'll check his reference. I'll let you know how it goes."

"You're the boss!"

Madison went up front to seat the lunch crowd. She wanted her customers to feel like they were being invited into a home. She enjoyed greeting people as they came in and the customers appreciated being welcomed by the owner. They felt valued and kept coming back.

She also helped bus tables, run orders, and poured coffee when she had a lull. Owning a café wasn't a glamorous lifestyle. She didn't even bother with makeup anymore, wearing a swipe of mascara and tinted lip balm. Any other makeup melted away while she worked. Her bin of cute summer sandals had gotten shoved into the back of the closet and rarely came out. Instead, she wore cushioned running shoes and went through several pairs a year.

The café stayed busy throughout the summer. Restaurant hours were 7:00 am – 9:00 pm, but they also catered special events. The summer calendar filled with weddings, family reunions, and various parties. This upcoming weekend there were two catering events, a Friday wedding and the Davises fiftieth anniversary on Saturday.

Staffing looked thin for the weekend, but it only took a few people to run catering. They offered buffet style meals and a bar service to keep things simple. It would be nice if Madison could hire more weekend staff, but they were able to make do with the current employees.

Her mind drifted without her realizing it until someone cleared their throat. Madison focused on the man in front of her and found herself drowning in stunning steel-blue eyes. Time seemed to slow until she slowly closed and then opened her own eyes, bringing reality down around her.

Madison smiled awkwardly. "I'm so sorry, I didn't hear you come in."

"No problem." His bright white smile seemed amused but understanding.

"Booth, table, or counter?" Madison reverted to routine while she tried to get a grip on herself.

He decided on a seat at the counter. Madison grabbed a menu and walked him over. "Have you been here before? You seem familiar, but I'm not sure I recognize you. Not that I know all the customers we have, but we get a lot of regulars around here." No matter how much her brain yelled shut up, Madison couldn't stop babbling. "We had quite the crowd this morning. Lots of our regulars were in for coffee. We always have a crowd at the door before we even open. Did you say you were from around here?" She paused long enough for him to answer.

"It's my first time here in the café. I've been to Cloud Lake a few times to visit my uncle and aunt."

She glanced up at him. He had to be six feet tall. He smelled nice, too, like cedar and leather. Madison's heart beat faster. Standing close to him felt strangely exhilarating.

"Maybe you know them? Andy and Molly Davis?" He asked as he slid into his chair.

"Yes, of course! We're catering for their party this weekend. Married fifty years! Isn't that amazing?" Madison willed herself to calm down. Why was her voice so high?

"Yes, it is." He gazed at her standing with the menu in hand.

Madison noticed him looking at her and flushed pink. "Here's our menu," she said, handing it over. "Our special today is tater-tot hotdish. Soup is vegetable beef. Your server is Rachel and she'll be right with you." Again, she found safety by slipping into her routine. It seemed to be the best choice. She let him settle in and rushed back to the host stand. Madison took a few deep gulps of air. What had gotten into her? She stared at him for a moment.

He was gorgeous, and his eyes were stunning. But his sandy blonde hair was too slicked back. He was wearing a polo and khaki shorts, which almost seemed too dressy. His air of confidence was too much. More importantly, it sounded like he was only here for the party. Basically, he was a tourist.

Madison dismissed him. She had to. There wasn't enough time in the day. She wouldn't waste a moment on an out-of-towner. He probably wasn't interested in her, anyway. She had acted like a teenager.

That covered enough excuses. She could come up with more later if she needed to. Taking one last deep breath, she willed her heart to slow to a more normal pace. More customers came through the door. She distracted herself by greeting them and getting them seated.

The lunch rush died out, but there would still be a steady trickle of people all afternoon. The older community would come in for more conversation, coffee, and possibly some pie. Families with young kids would come in to get a break from the sun and have ice cream treats or an early dinner. Teenagers would come in together with their sunburnt noses stuck in their phones, giggling and having milkshakes or fries.

Madison took a fresh pot of coffee and made her way through the dining room. She asked the new customers dining how they were doing. She stopped and chatted with the people she knew.

"How are my favorite fishermen today?" Madison made her first stop.

They greeted her with rounds of "Good. Good." and satisfied nods.

"Good morning for bass fishing," Lenny said.

"Too bad you didn't catch any!" Frank said, followed by a loud belly laugh. "All he caught today was a handful of sunfish. They were barely big enough to keep!"

Ted broke in, "We should have fished over on Long Lake if you wanted bass."

Madison knew they were on the verge of another epic debate. "I think you're all full of fish tales! Have a great afternoon, fellas." They all chuckled at her, and she moved on.

At the next table, Mindy kept her kids occupied with kid's menus and colors. Madison and Mindy met in their seventh-grade English class and had been friends ever since. Mindy married her sweetheart right after high school graduation. Madison wondered what it was like to be so certain about someone and if she'd ever find that. They spent a few minutes catching up before Mindy had to leave to get her youngest down for a nap.

Madison was ready for her favorite table. They came in every Tuesday for lunch before they went for their once-a-week grocery shop. They ordered the same thing every week. He asked for the walleye sandwich and fries. She asked for the chicken salad sandwich and a cup of homestyle vegetable beef soup. Madison grabbed a burger, fries and a root beer and joined them.

"Beautiful girl!" he still greeted her the same way he had since she was a little girl.

"Grandpa, how are you doing today?"

Grandma Mabel spoke right up, not letting Grandpa Don answer for himself. "He's fit as a fiddle. He had his checkup last Wednesday, you know. Though the doctor did say he should lose some weight and maybe not eat so many fries."

Grandpa let out a snort and protested. "He did not!"

"He did so!" said Grandma Mabel, not willing to be outdone. "Doctor Lee said to stay away from fat and salt. That's what fries are! Fat and salt!"

Madison eyed her plate. "But Grandma, they're so delicious!" she took a fry and popped it into her mouth.

"Oh, you're as bad as he is!"

Madison cherished her Tuesday lunch with her grandparents. She knew she should spend more time with them, but the restaurant consumed so much of her time. They were busy too. They were active in the community, gardened and hiked. Recently, they had purchased e-bikes and rode all over the trails around the lake.

"How is your dad's old truck running for you?" Grandpa finally broke into the conversation.

She assured Grandpa Don she checked the oil regularly and made sure the tires had enough air pressure. He didn't have as much to say as Grandma Mabel, but Madison suspected he could hardly get a word in edgewise.

And that was all that would be said about her parents. A mention so that everyone would keep remembering their existence, but not so much their grief would overwhelm them. Sometimes she wished they would say something more and talk about their memories out loud. Madison wanted to talk about the emptiness she felt inside. Her grandparents exchanged a look, and her grandmother drew her back into a conversation about a sale on summer peaches.

Lunch ended too soon, and Madison had to get back to work. She walked her grandparents over to the door. She hugged her grandma first.

"Now don't work too hard!" Grandma Mabel patted her hand.

"I'll try not to, Grandma, but it's a hard habit to break!"

She hugged her grandpa. He leaned in and kissed her cheek.

So quiet she barely heard him, he spoke. "Love you, girl. Find yourself someone to fancy, will you?"

Madison laughed quietly to herself as she walked back to the counter. Where had Grandpa come up with that one? She glanced at the blue-eyed man sitting at the counter and bit her lip. It really was too bad he was from out of town.

CHAPTER 4

At the counter, Ryan nursed his iced tea. He had finished his lunch, but he couldn't talk himself into leaving. There was still time to kill before he could get into his rental, and he had nothing else to do. He took another glance at the hostess. She made her way through the dining room with another fresh pot of coffee.

Ryan lived in a different world. Where some of the women were sleek, chic, and ready to do business. They brokered high powered deals, ran multi-billion-dollar companies and were members on prestigious boards. A relationship with one of them seemed more like a business deal than an adventure in love.

Others spent too much time in the salon hoping their polished plastic looks would land them the millionaire of their dreams. They lived off family money and didn't have a care in the world. He wanted more than they had to offer him.

Something about this woman intrigued him. She looked good in her café T-shirt and jean shorts. He couldn't explain it, but he liked what he saw. She seemed down to earth, warm, and friendly. He wanted to get to know her.

"Need anything else here? Fresh strawberry pie? Hot fudge sundae?" His server, Rachel, seemed to be one of the youngest on staff.

"No, thank you." He flashed a bright smile at her, and she giggled.

"Actually, there is something." He leaned in like he was about to share a secret with the girl. "Can you tell me what her name is?"

Rachel tossed her long, dark hair over her shoulder as she turned to see who Ryan meant. "That's Madison. Did you need her for something? I can get her for you."

"No. I don't need anything. I just wanted to know her name."

"All righty, here's the check. You can pay me here when you're ready. Do you need a refill at all?"

"No, I'll be on my way shortly." He handed her a black metal credit card and finished his tea.

Ryan couldn't help himself. He took one last look at the hostess. It seemed so silly, but when she had gazed into his eyes, he felt like they experienced a connection. He wasn't here looking for romance, but he wasn't against the idea. Smiling to himself, he put on his sunglasses and went out into the bright sunshine. He expected the rest of the week at Cloud Lake to be a good one. He couldn't wait to have another lunch at the Sunflower Café. Tomorrow he might have to stay for that slice of pie.

He climbed into his Escalade and pulled up directions to the cabin he had rented. His brother would join him tomorrow. His dad would come the day after. Ryan wanted to check in before them. He needed to unwind before they arrived. After wrapping up a mess of a deal at work, an extra day to relax seemed justified. He would clear his head and refocus before they arrived. There was big news to share with them and they would not like it.

He was done. He was done with expensive suits and silk ties. He was done with endless meetings and demanding clients. He was done with city life. He was done doing what was expected of him. He was one high-powered deal away from a nervous breakdown and he knew it. It was time to leave that lifestyle behind.

Ryan had to focus. One last deal lay on the table. A simple deal, but a significant one. Instead of chasing after wealth, he would chase his dreams. It would disappoint his father, no question about that. His uncle had gone through the same thing with the family. They didn't understand when Uncle Andy quit his corporate job and moved his family out to lake country to run a small resort.

The family would never admit it, but his uncle embarrassed them. They turned their noses up at the modest cabins and fishing boats rentals. They couldn't get over the fact that he drove a secondhand Jeep and bought his clothes from a discount department store. Sending his kids to public school seemed like a terrible idea. Everyone else in the family attended private or even boarding schools.

Ryan's father, Scott, felt obligated to attend his uncle's fiftieth wedding anniversary. He refused to stay at the resort and insisted they rent a lake house. His original plan included renting three lake houses, one for each of them, but there weren't enough suitable rentals on Cloud Lake. They would be spread out to the other lakes in the region if they didn't bunk together. Ryan eventually found a rental so outrageous that even his father agreed to it.

He pulled into a driveway that ended in an impressive lake house. He took out his suitcase and briefcase and made his way up the walkway. He punched in the code the rental agent had given him and opened the heavy, ornate door.

"This is ridiculous," Ryan thought as he let himself in. "You would think we were staying in the Hamptons."

The lake home was larger than his home in the city. The main area had a large living room, updated designer kitchen and an elegant main suite. There were two wings, each with their own bedroom suites. The basement boasted a game room, a personal movie theater that was hidden behind a bookcase, and a two-lane bowling alley.

The rental came with daily housekeeping and shopping services. The kitchen had been fully stocked with the food and beverages he'd requested. Floor to ceiling windows revealed a spectacular view of the lake. Off the deck sat a twelve-person hot tub and sauna. Down at the docks, there would be a speedboat and several jet skis.

Homes of this caliber were a rarity in the county. This one seemed out of place compared to the homes he could see dotting the shoreline around the lake. Most of the cabins were fairly modest. From his research, he knew that many of them didn't even have a furnace. People used them for the summer months and closed up long before the first snow. They provided a place to sleep as people escaped from city life for the weekends. They didn't spend time in their cabins, they spent their time outside enjoying nature.

Ryan brought his suitcase and briefcase into one of the bedroom suites and promptly unpacked, hanging his clothes in the walk-in closet. He hardly noticed his surroundings. The rooms were quite large. They were decorated with tasteful pine and soft leather, giving the room a comfortable atmosphere.

The briefcase containing his laptop went on the desk. Ryan knew he'd have to open it before too long, whether he wanted to or not. Before he did, he wanted a cold beer and some warm sunshine. Making his way to the refrigerator, he grabbed a bottle and went out to the patio. He sank into the cushions of one of the wooden Adirondack chairs, kicked off his shoes, and pulled off his shirt, revealing his muscular chest and tight abs. He took a long drink of the cold beer and breathed a sigh of relief.

Could life be like this? Ryan had traveled to exotic and interesting places over the years, but this was incredibly peaceful. He took in a deep breath of the fresh country air while he admired the view. A family of loons swam slowly by on the soft waves of the lake. Birds chirped away, happily making up songs from the trees. And the foliage – gigantic oaks with the greenest canopy of leaves he had ever seen surrounded the lake. The wind rustled through them softly. Immersed in the moment, he jumped when his phone buzzed with an incoming call.

Ryan frowned as he pulled it out of his back pocket. He almost didn't answer it when his dad flashed on the caller ID.

"Hi Dad."

"Hey Son. Are you all settled in?"

Ryan was skeptical of his father's cheerful tone and polite question. Scott Davis may sound as if he cared about Ryan getting settled, but Ryan knew this call had a purpose. His father worried about his own comfort. Ryan didn't bother to fake niceties with him and instead began his report.

"The lake home is as nice as the website claims. I left you the main suite. They stocked the kitchen with everything we asked for. You'll be comfortable here." Ryan sounded like a soldier. He gazed out at the loons on the water. The baby swam close to the parents, and you could hardly see it. "I'm out on the patio having a beer." He added the little tidbit as an afterthought. He half shrugged to himself as he listened to his dad.

"Good. I'm glad everything is in order. We're booked for a round of golf after I arrive."

"Fine." Ryan noticed his dad ignored the patio comment.

"See you then, Son." His father hung up before Ryan could say goodbye.

He stared hard at the screen. His phone buzzed again. This time, a text from his boss came through.

Good job on the Casswell deal. Let's talk Monday.

Monday. He'd be back in the city. Back in his house. Going to the office. He texted back.

Stuck in meetings most of the morning, but free in the afternoon.

Let's do a late lunch at Sylvester's. 2:00 pm.

I'll put it on my calendar.

Ryan's phone buzzed again. He considered throwing it into the lake. Instead, he put on a smile that didn't entirely reach his eyes and answered the call. He spent the afternoon answering calls, texts, and emails.

His out-of-office messages directed clients to several of his colleagues who should be able to handle any issues during his absence. It seemed useless. He could turn off his phone and ignore them, but the problems would remain and would make a bigger mess to clean up next week. He might as well put in a day of work and try to keep his to-do list under control.

After a long afternoon of working from the patio, Ryan didn't feel like cooking. He abandoned his original plan of grilling salmon and a potato. Late into the evening, he made a sandwich with chips and cracked open another beer. He turned on the 10 o'clock news and sank into the couch. He started scrolling through his phone, but it didn't feel right. He turned the television off and put his phone on Do Not Disturb.

The quiet and dark had a calming effect on him. He could hear crickets and frogs through the screen door on the patio. The stress of the day melted away. He glanced out at the night sky dotted with bright stars and decided to turn in early. It only took a moment for him to fall asleep.

Ryan slept better than he had in months. In the morning, he sat up and stretched. He thought about reaching for his phone but changed his mind. Instead, he grabbed some clothes and running shoes. The cabin came equipped with a personal gym in the basement, but the outdoors called to him.

He preferred to run outside. Running on the treadmill reminded him of a hamster running on a wheel. He never put on music or the news. He took the opportunity to be alone with his thoughts. His best ideas and many solutions to his problems often came to him during his runs.

His mind felt muddled as he started to run. If he had thought it through, he would have run north. On his return trip, the sun would be out of his eyes.

Something other than intense morning sunshine entered his thoughts, or rather some*one*. He thought about honey-blond hair piled in a messy bun, eyes the blue of water on a sunny day and a warm, sweet smile. There was someone he couldn't wait to see again. His running shoes headed west.

CHAPTER 5

Madison did not wake in a good mood. The previous day had stressed her out. She even had a server call out for the evening shift and ended up staying until close to help cover. Her plan to watch a movie after her shift fizzled out when her internet quit working.

She struggled with her grumpy mood. Madison preferred to have her Wednesdays off, if at all possible. Showering didn't rinse away the clouds. Drying her hair didn't blow them along either. Getting dressed in her work clothes certainly didn't help. She grabbed her apron and car keys and headed out to her old truck.

Dawn broke as she drove out to the café. She pulled over to the side of the road to take in the view. The sunrise over the lake boasted brilliant shades of pink, orange, and purple. Rolling down her window, she listened to the morning unfold. A duck quacked nearby, and Madison realized she must have parked too close to a nest. She put the truck in gear and drove the rest of the way to the café.

Her mood lightened as she pulled into the parking lot. Looking into her rearview mirror, she piled her hair into a messy bun. She grabbed a lip balm out of the ashtray and swiped it across her lips. She tried motivating herself to face the day, telling herself it would be wonderful, and she couldn't wait to get started. The old truck door creaked as she threw it open and hopped out.

Movement caught her eye and she thought it might be a deer. She glanced at the road and saw a figure run by. It was the guy – the tall, tan and handsome guy whose steely blue eyes she swam in yesterday. With his shirt off, his body glowed golden in the morning sun. His muscles rippled with every step. He looped through the laundromat parking lot next door and ran back towards her.

He saw her, smiled, and waved. She blushed furiously and raised a hand to wave back, embarrassed to be caught staring. A fire stirred inside Madison. She stood for a moment, admiring him as he ran along the road.

Madison forgot her bad mood. She unlocked the back door and flipped on light switches. Humming to herself, she made her way through the kitchen to the front of the restaurant. She started her morning routine, brewing the coffee and getting her mug ready while it perked. No working until after the first sip. She decided today might indeed be a good day.

She heard the back door open and went into the kitchen.

"Good morning, Benny."

"Good morning, sunshine. Are you ready to have a fabulous day?"

"Yes, I'd love to have a fabulous day. How about you?"

"Every day is a good day to have a good day! Hey, did you hear what the coffee reported to the police?"

Madison grinned at him. "No, what did the coffee report to the police?"

"That they were mugged."

"Hilarious." Madison turned to walk away.

"I could tell a joke about a pizza, but it's a little cheesy."

"I'm going into my office now!" Madison yelled over her shoulder. She went up front to grab her mug of coffee before she settled in and turned on her computer. She worked on finishing staff schedules until Chloe popped her head in with the coffeepot.

"Good morning." Chloe sounded terrible.

Madison looked up from the screen. "Are you all right?"

"Is it that obvious?"

"Is what obvious? Chloe, what's wrong?"

"My heart is broken. Smashed into pieces."

"Again? Are you going to refill my mug? I'll need a fresh cup for this."

"Oh. Yeah." Chloe perked up again. She topped off Madison's mug and filled her own. "It's not like it happens every day, you know."

"Chloe, I don't even remember this one's name. How long have you been dating?"

"His name was Nathan. We dated almost a month! And what am I supposed to do tomorrow? I don't have a date now!"

"I don't have a date either. It will still be fun."

"But..."

Madison put up her hand and stopped Chloe. "It is supposed to be ninety degrees and sunny. I have stocked up on seltzers, beer, and bottled water. I haven't had a chance to go tubing in years.

We're not going to let a guy, someone who probably wasn't worth your time in the first place, ruin a perfectly fun day."

Chloe stared at Madison like she was out of her mind. After a moment, a smile tugged at the corners of her mouth, and she nodded. "You're right, as usual."

"Damn straight I am. Now let's get to work! We've got customers waiting!"

Madison pepped herself up for the team meeting and her staff caught on to her enthusiasm. They were all ready to have a good morning. Madison made her way to the front to unlock the door, letting her stream of regulars in to find their seats.

The crowd stood patiently at the entrance, waiting to come in. Behind them stood a couple that looked good together and knew it. The woman had beautiful olive skin, shiny dark hair, manicured nails, and immaculate makeup. Next to her stood a tall man with dark eyes, brown skin, and blue-black hair.

When he saw her, he put on a dazzling smile. "Good morning, Madison. I wondered if you were working today."

If Madison could have left the building, she would have. "Jonah. What a surprise. Having breakfast with us today?"

"Yes, can we get a booth?"

Madison led the way. She glanced away while they slid into the same side of the booth. He placed his arm around the girl and stared at Madison.

"This is my girlfriend, Kassidy."

"Nice to meet you, Kassidy." Madison didn't bother looking at either of them. "Chloe will be with you in a moment."

"Aw, aren't you going to wait on us? Like the good old days?"

"Chloe will take great care of you. Enjoy your breakfast."

Madison went into the wait station to get a glass of water. Her mouth went dry when Jonah had walked in. She wished she could kick him out, but her parents had raised her to mind her manners. When it came to the restaurant, etiquette could make or break the business.

"Is that who I think it is?" Chloe snuck up beside her.

"Yep. It's Jonah." Madison didn't like saying his name. She hadn't said it out loud since the night before her parents' funeral. He had broken up with her. He'd made excuses: he was too young, he couldn't handle it all. She had cried his name and asked him not to leave her. He had walked out her front door and driven off in his Camaro.

In hindsight, she could see it was for the best, but the wound hadn't healed.

"What is he doing here?"

"I don't know. I didn't ask him. I don't really want to know."

"Well, I better go see if he wants coffee."

"Leave it be for once. Okay, Chloe?"

Chloe put her arm around Madison in a quick hug. "You got it, boss."

Madison made a beeline for her office, hoping to hide out there. She found a little paperwork to do and caught up on the small pile of papers that needed filing. She stared at her computer, trying to find something to work on. There was nothing left. She made her way into the kitchen to see if anything needed to be done there. Nothing could be cleaned while the cooks were making food. She did a few racks of dishes, but that didn't take long either. She wandered over to Benny and he looked at her from his place at the grill.

"What?"

"Need anything, Benny?"

"A million dollars and a vacation in Tahiti."

"Anything else?"

"It's all under control."

"Sounds good. Let me know if you need me."

Madison sighed. There was nothing to do. She might as well go chat with the regulars and help the servers if they needed anything. On her way into the dining room, she grabbed a coffeepot.

She spotted the Cloud Lake Summer Lovin' Club. The book club met at the café every week during the summer and read steamy romance novels.

"Madison! What are you doing here on a Wednesday? We haven't seen you in forever." The leader of the group, Jessica, asked.

"Tonya wanted the day off. Her son and his family are coming in later today."

"I completely forgot!" Jessica said. "I've been so into this book. The romance. The drama. This guy and his snake hips!"

Madison took a moment to picture that one. "What are snake hips?"

"I don't know, but I like them!"

The women around the table laughed and bobbed their heads in agreement. Madison shook her head and smiled as she left the table.

She paused at a few more tables to chat but avoided the area where Jonah and his girlfriend were sitting. There was no sense rubbing salt into old wounds. She ran out of coffee and went to brew more. Jonah and Kassidy stood up to leave. He smiled at her and waved on his way out of the door.

Chloe came over. "Can you believe that guy? Coming in here?"

"Yes. I can." Madison said and sighed.

"While they were eating, he kept telling his girlfriend stories about you."

"Are you serious? What did she say?"

"She didn't say much of anything. They're a strange couple."

"Did he say why he came in?"

"I told you I would stay out of it. I didn't ask."

"I didn't think you would actually listen to me."

Chloe struck one of her signature poses. "I'm hurt you think so little of me!"

"I think the world of you, my friend."

"Well, in that case. I didn't ask him, but he told me. He's back in town for a friend's wedding. He said he tells Kassidy about this place all the time and wanted to bring her here. Seeing you was the icing on the cake."

"And she didn't say anything?"

"She rolled her eyes and told him she was bored."

"Wow. Sounds like a great relationship."

"I think you dodged a bullet with that guy."

"I know I did, but it still stings."

Chloe studied her with thoughtful eyes. "Things are under control in here. Why don't you take a break and have an early lunch? Or a late breakfast? Have you even eaten today?"

Madison thought about it. "Hm, nope. I've had coffee. I guess I better go bug Benny for something to eat."

She had him throw down some chicken strips and fries. She made herself a strawberry shake while she waited for her food to come up. When Benny hollered for her, she grabbed her plate and headed out the back door. Usually she ate in her office, but she needed some fresh air. She set her food in her truck bed, lowered the gate, and hopped up. She ate her lunch while soaking up the sun's warmth and watching little waves of the lake lap the shore.

Customers often asked why she didn't have a patio on the side of the restaurant facing the lake. The windows were nice, but they wanted to sit outside to watch the water and sit in the sun. She had researched adding one, but zoning laws and red tape made it impossible. The Sunflower Café was what it was. Secretly, she appreciated that it wouldn't change. She had an entire life of memories tied up in the restaurant.

Madison took a deep breath of sweet summer air before heading inside. She smiled a wry smile at the thoughts tumbling through her head. Part of her pushed so hard for something more, but a bigger part of her stayed stuck in the past. She wanted to move forward but wasn't entirely sure she could move on.

CHAPTER 6

*R*yan's thoughts wandered back to his morning run. More truthfully, he kept thinking about the woman from the café, Madison. He had hoped to see her but hadn't thought he actually would. He didn't notice her when he ran past the restaurant, but when he looped around to head back to the lake house she was standing right there. The rising sun illuminated her figure, and she returned his wave. He couldn't wait to see her again when he went to the café for lunch.

"It's on my radar. It seems like the Paradis Parsa Building will be the low hanging fruit. What do you think, Ryan?"

What did he think? He wasn't even supposed to be on this call. "Hal, I think you've got a good handle on the situation. Thanks for taking care of things while I'm on vacation."

Another voice broke in. "That's great. We'll have to wrap this up for today. I've got another meeting to get to." Jenyssa called an end to the meeting. Ryan appreciated her *time is money* attitude, especially when she ruled her meetings with an iron fist. She wasn't about to let Hal waste everyone's time with his posturing and platitudes.

Ryan stretched out in his chair. He might have resigned himself to working on his vacation, but the morning was too beautiful to waste. It was too early for a beer, but a cup of coffee seemed like a good idea. He went into the lake house and started the coffee maker. He opened the refrigerator and looked inside, but he wasn't really hungry. He shut the door again and walked over to the windows.

There were jet skis down at the dock. The day was warming up. It would feel wonderful to get out on the water for a while. He went back to his bedroom and changed into swimming trunks. He grabbed his cup of coffee from the kitchen and went out on the deck to figure things out. He pulled up the lake house reservation information on his laptop.

The rental agreement had a few guidelines for using the watercraft: must be 18 to operate, state law requires the use of life vests, do not operate under the influence of drugs or alcohol. There was a short "how to" of sorts. Lifejackets were stored in the shed by the dock. The keys for the watercraft were in a key cabinet by the patio door. He went back in and found the "key" to the jet ski. It was a small plastic piece attached to a wristlet with a coil of cord.

He put the wristlet on and walked down to find the shed. It was full of supplies. Besides the lifejackets of assorted sizes, there were skis, wakeboards, kneeboards, floaties, and an assortment of beach and water toys. He found a bright yellow jacket in his size and went to check out the jet ski. He'd never ridden one before, but it seemed easy enough. There didn't seem to be a place for the key though.

Ryan went back to the patio to see if there were further instructions. There weren't any. He wasn't about to give up and after a quick internet search, he found a video on how to ride a jet ski Sipping his coffee, he watched it intently.

He laughed at himself when the person in the video showed how to use the key. They slid it around a notched cylinder on top of the steering system. He watched a few videos of people getting flung off their jet skis, which showed the engine would automatically shut off if the key slid off the cylinder.

Realizing he couldn't do an internet search while he was out on the water, he watched more videos of how to operate the jet ski. Then he looked up the state laws to make sure he wasn't missing anything. Almost an hour later, he felt prepared enough to take the jet ski out on the lake.

He went back out on the dock, put the lifejacket on, and lowered the lift. Once the jet ski was in the water he gingerly stepped onto the rail and swung his other leg over the seat. He was relieved the thing didn't topple over on him. It took a few moments to look over the controls, but there wasn't much to it. He slid the key into the notch and pressed start.

Slowly he gave it some gas and moved forward. He drove away from the dock and out onto the open water. There wasn't much traffic on the lake, just a few boats with people fishing in them. He stayed away from them and followed the shoreline while he got used to driving the jet ski.

Ryan gained confidence and gave it more gas. He let the wind whip around him as he traveled across the water. It felt exhilarating. Before he realized it, there was a boat coming towards him. Was he supposed to go left or right? He jerked the handlebars to turn and whipped himself right off the jet ski. He erupted in laughter until water went up his nose and he started to splutter.

He climbed back on the machine and shook his head to help dry out his hair. He slid the key back on and hoped the jet ski would start. It roared back into life. He got his bearings and started back towards the cabin.

A group of teenagers on jet skis sped past him. They took turns jumping the wake the front jet ski left behind. Then they spun around in circles creating large waves. They drove out of the turbulent water, turned around and drove back through it. He could hear their cheers and screams as they jumped the waves they had created.

It looked too fun to not try it. He spun his own machine in circles, drove out of the waves, whipped around, and drove back into them. His jet ski dipped, rode up on a wave and crashed down sideways. Again, he was thrown into the water. This time he made sure to surface before letting the laughter escape him.

One of the teenagers drove over to check on him. "Mister, are you all right?"

Ryan couldn't stop laughing. He climbed back onto the jet ski. "That was fun. How do you guys stay on when you go through the waves?"

The kid laughed. "You have to hold on tight. Use your guns, man." The kid flexed an arm and laughed again before taking off and leaving Ryan in his wake.

The wind and water felt good in the hot sunshine. Ryan played on the water until his arms ached. He had to give it up and brought the jet ski back. He managed to get it onto the lift and himself back onto the dock. He left his lifejacket on the deck to let it dry out and returned the key to the cabinet. Feeling dehydrated from his fun in the sun, he pulled a bottle of water from the refrigerator and drank it down.

His arms were going to be sore later, but it would be worth it. That was more fun than he'd had in ages. Laughter bubbled up again as he remembered the feeling of being airborne before slapping into the water. Jet skiing was a rush, and he would definitely get out on the water again soon.

Ryan needed another shower. He'd already taken one after his morning run, but he would need to get cleaned up again before he went to lunch. He checked his cell phone and saw a half dozen messages from Hal and several missed calls. His shower would have to wait. It seemed like Hal was on a rampage.

Before he could even read the messages, Hal called again.

"Hello, Hal. What's up?"

Hal didn't bother with a greeting. "Can you believe her? She cut the meeting short before we even got into the Paradis Parsa building."

"You called me to talk about Jenyssa?"

"No, I called you to talk about the P and P!"

"Right, what's the issue here Hal?"

Hal sighed. "Ryan, I realize you're technically on vacation..."

Ryan grimaced.

"But you of all people should realize how lucrative this deal could be."

Ryan knew at this point, anything he said would be taken the wrong way. He let Hal rant about the possibilities of the deal, what could go wrong, and how no one was listening to him. Ryan assured him he was listening.

Hal snorted. "Of course you are. You understand where I'm coming from, don't you son?"

Son? Ryan wondered what Hal was really angling for. There were rumors that the board members weren't happy with Hal's performance the past year or so. Was this call a political maneuver?

"I understand you perfectly, Hal."

Ryan let Hal ramble on for several minutes to make sure there wasn't anything that actually needed his attention. When the conversation looped back to Jenyssa, Ryan cut Hal short.

"Look, I'll be back in the office Monday. Why don't we find a time next week to call a meeting? Nothing is going to happen with the P and P before then."

Hal settled for a meeting, but insisted Ryan set it up. Ryan agreed to look at their calendars that afternoon and find a suitable time. "Pick your battles" came to mind when Ryan dealt with difficult coworkers or customers. Sometimes it was worth standing your ground, but this was not one of those times.

He plugged his phone in to charge and skimmed through his other messages and emails. Nothing else was urgent enough to distract him. It was time to get cleaned up. He took a hot shower, hoping to avoid some of the aches and pains that would surely set in later. After toweling off, he slicked back his hair and got dressed in a polo and khaki shorts.

Ryan heard his phone buzz. He took it off the charger and looked at the incoming call. It was Jenyssa.

"Christ, did Hal call you?"

"Hello, Jenyssa."

"I don't have time for pleasantries, Ryan. He's been talking to anyone who will listen. I don't know what he's trying to pull, but I'm not letting him drag me down with him on this one."

Ryan tried to listen to what Jenyssa was explaining, but he couldn't concentrate. Apparently, this P and P deal would make or break somebody in the office. If he had to bet on anyone coming out on top, it would be Jenyssa, but he couldn't understand why they kept dragging him into it.

Before he could figure out what she wanted from him, Jenyssa said her goodbyes and hung up. He glared at his phone. If he could, he would stick the two of them into a room until they could get along. When you dealt with multimillion-dollar properties and high-profile clients, there was no room for error. If it got out that there were conflicts happening behind the scenes, they could easily lose out on the deal. People got skittish when that kind of money was on the line.

He sat down with his laptop. He needed to read through his messages and emails and see if he had to get involved any further. After catching up, he realized that there wasn't anything he could do, especially while he was on vacation.

Ryan set up the meeting he had agreed to. He composed another email, reiterating that he was on vacation and that he would be available the following Monday. It wouldn't stop the work from coming in, but maybe it would slow things down.

There were more important things to think about, like what kind of pie the café would have available at lunch and if he'd get a chance to talk to Madison. He might even take advantage of his time at Cloud Lake and ask her out on a date. An evening with her would be a great distraction from everything going on.

CHAPTER 7

Madison put on her game face as she walked through the kitchen. The morning had rattled her more than she cared to admit, but she could easily fix her mood. She threw herself back into her work and moved on. She needed to cover part of the counter at lunch and she hoped the lunch rush would keep her busy.

Madison walked to the doorway between the kitchen and wait station. The hostess came to get her.

"Hi Madison, there's a lady up front with an application."

Madison glanced at her watch: 10:45. It wasn't quite time for the café to go crazy. "I have time, I'll talk to her."

The girl standing by the host stand seemed familiar to Madison. She tried to place the girl's long brown hair and bright green eyes, but it didn't come to her. She walked over to the girl, noted how short she stood, and extended her hand. "Hello, I'm Madison. You have an application to turn in?"

"Hi Madison. I'm Leah. Here's the application. Are you hiring?"

"Yes, I am. Do you have time now for an interview?"

"That would be great."

Madison offered her a drink, but Leah declined. They slid into a booth and Madison scanned her application.

"Why don't you tell me a little about yourself?"

"Sure. I was born and raised here. I went to college in the cities for a year, but I'll be honest with you, it just wasn't for me. So, I got a job serving at a 24-hour diner. I've been there for three years, and I liked it there a lot, but my dad is having some health trouble. My mom asked me to come home to help take care of him."

"Wait a minute, are you Corey and Lana Gordon's daughter?"

"Yes."

"I thought I recognized you. This might be the fastest interview I've had in a while. If you want the serving spot, it's yours."

They discussed hours and wages. Leah accepted the position and agreed to start on Friday. Chloe would go over paperwork and get her trained in. Madison walked her back to the door.

"I'm sorry to hear about your dad, but I'm looking forward to having you on our team."

"Thanks Madison. I'll see you Friday!"

Madison joined Chloe behind the counter. "You didn't come over."

"Didn't have to. I told Leah to apply in the first place," Chloe grinned.

"I should have known."

"My parents and her parents play cards together. She's a nice girl. Did you hire her?"

"Yes, but don't tell Benny. He's a little upset I didn't hire Landon right away."

"Are you going to hire him?"

"Probably." Madison absently nodded her head. "But on some sort of trial. We'll see how the dishes survive before I decide to keep him on."

"That's great news! We'll be a full house again." When she didn't get a response, Chloe's eyes searched Madison's face. "Are you okay?"

"Hm? I'm fine. This morning has been all over the place, though. I feel scattered."

"Well, buckle up, buttercup. Here comes the crowd!" Chloe patted her on the back and went to wait on her customers.

Madison had customers to greet as well and looked forward to the distraction. A group of construction workers sat at the counter.

"Hey guys. Hey Dylan. You missed breakfast today."

"Amy stayed up all night with D.J. I brought him to daycare for her. Then he spit up all over and I had to change my shirt. I had to settle for gas station coffee and a donut."

"You poor dear. Good thing you had time to come in for lunch today."

"Only because our lumber delivery is late. It didn't come in this morning and now they're saying it will be late afternoon."

"Can't catch a break today, can you? You want the usual? Double bacon cheeseburger, fries, and coleslaw?"

"You got it. Thanks Madison."

"My pleasure."

Madison busied herself waiting on her customers and helping the other servers. She was leaning shoulder deep in the cooler, scooping ice cream for a shake, when she got the feeling there were eyes on her. She set the shake cup under the blender, fired it up, and glanced over at the counter. There he was again. Was she going to see this guy all the time now?

Chloe came over to pour a glass of iced tea. "I see you staring at him. He sure ticks your boxes. Tall, tan, handsome, and then some. I tried flirting with this one, but his eyes keep wandering over to you!"

"He is pretty cute." Madison tried to sound cool, but inside, those tiny flames were heating up. She walked off to deliver the shake. Her stride seemed to change. Somehow, it became more feminine and awkward all at the same time. She detoured to make a round of the dining room to take a moment. It was silly acting like a teenager with a crush. She was a grown woman, a businesswoman, and would soon be an entrepreneur.

She returned to the counter. Chloe joined her there and put her hand on her hip. "Madison!"

"What?"

"Just because a man isn't from here, doesn't mean he's a terrible person."

Madison made an effort to keep from rolling her eyes. "I'm sure he's wonderful. Fabulous. Fantastic. But it's busy and you have a new table."

Chloe shook her head and walked off to wait on her customers. Madison went to clear off the counter spots where customers had left. She tried to ignore the guy but noticed him studying her while she worked.

Finally, he spoke up, "I thought you were a hostess. Today you're a waitress?"

"Hostess, waitress, dishwasher, cook, manager, and owner." Madison couldn't help herself and smiled. She loved his voice, smooth and deep. She hoped she wasn't blushing again.

"Owner? The café is yours?" Ryan seemed impressed.

"Sure is. My dad owned it. I grew up playing Barbies in the back booths and sneaking fries from the cooks."

"I should have guessed. You were the first one here this morning."

"Oh, right, you were out running."

Madison flushed. Thinking of him glowing in the first light of the day woke her up and stirred up feelings. It wasn't right. She was not interested. Just because Grandpa had told her to find someone to fancy didn't mean she had to fancy the first person to come along!

"I'm Ryan." He said, flashing a brilliant smile.

"I'm Madison." Her smile betrayed her awkwardness. "So, what do you do, Ryan?"

"That's a hard question to answer right now. The best answer is I'm in commercial real estate."

"Sounds complicated."

"It is sometimes."

She cut the conversation short. "I have to…"

"Look, I know you have to get back to work, but would you care to go out for dinner or drinks? I'm here through Sunday if you have an evening free."

Time stood still for Madison. Her heart thumped faster. It said yes, Yes, YES! She found herself drowning in those eyes again.

Madison licked her lips. "I'm sorry, I don't have time. Thank you, but no."

She beat a hasty retreat to her office.

Chloe found her grabbing her keys. "Need me to take over your customers?"

"Damn. Yes, Chloe. I don't know where my head is today. I'm going to the bank for my appointment."

"I'm on it."

"You're the best, Chloe. I'll be back."

Madison left out the back door and jumped into her truck. She started it up but took a moment to decide her next step. Her appointment wasn't for an hour. It was too early to show up there. She rubbed her eyes and adjusted her messy bun. She decided on a drive around the lake. Putting the truck into gear, she pulled out of the parking lot.

"Men," she muttered to herself. "Grandpa must be nuts. Find someone to fancy." Madison shook her head. "See what happened with Jonah."

Madison had seen all the signs that he wasn't a great guy, but she had been so into him. They had a whirlwind romance. He brought her flowers, opened doors for her, and made a great impression on her parents. Then everything changed. He criticized her weight and what she ate. If she didn't call him back fast enough or tell him she loved him often enough, he picked fights with her. When she talked about her future, he laughed and said no wife of his was going to have a career.

Leaving her the day before her parents' funeral had been the worst. Madison thought he would be by her side in the church pew, holding her hand during the service. She wanted him next to her at the gravesite with his arm around her for support. He left her to deal with everything on her own and the betrayal wounded her deeply.

Not to mention, there were whispers he ran around on her. She hadn't believed them, but two days after the funeral, she saw him with another girl. It rubbed salt in her wounded heart.

Madison wondered why he had come into the restaurant. He acted like she was some old friend from high school instead of his ex-girlfriend. She couldn't fathom what he was up to or why he would involve his current girlfriend.

As she rounded the north corner of the lake, her thoughts turned to Ryan. Her cheeks burned with embarrassment. At least she had been polite when she turned him down. She meant to say yes, but she couldn't make the words come out right. Maybe it was for the best. Madison enjoyed her comfortable life. She did what she wanted and didn't answer to anyone else.

Madison didn't need anyone else. If she couldn't fix her leaky sink, she could hire someone to take care of it for her. She would not settle with another relationship. If she couldn't have what her parents had and what her grandparents still had, she didn't want it.

She drove by the resort and thought about stopping. She chewed her lip. The realtor had worried her yesterday. It was only a few more days until everything would be ready. Surely she would have heard if someone else was interested in the place.

There was no real need to stop. She could picture every inch of the place in her mind. The line of cabins, the tall oak trees, and the wide grassy area where she would build the event center. She would focus on her plans, not the men that drove her crazy.

The event center would keep her busy. She could picture it clearly. It would have deep rich wood, stone accents, and soft glowing lights. She imagined a wedding with a beautiful smiling couple surrounded by loved ones and friends. Or a family reunion like Andy and Molly planned. Instead of holding it in the dark service club or risking the chance of rain, they could have a beautiful, bright place to bring everyone.

Daydreaming didn't relieve the tension. Madison worried too much about problems she had no control over. She turned to drive to the bank. Maybe the banker could meet with her early. If not, the cool, quiet atmosphere in the bank would help calm her nerves.

CHAPTER 8

*T*hat did not go as planned. Ryan stared at Madison as she retreated to the kitchen.

Thank you, but no.

Had anyone ever turned him down for a date before? Ryan thought back. He couldn't think of one single time. He'd broken up with women, of course, and a few had broken up with him. His relationships never seemed to last longer than six months before boredom set in. This time, he felt there had been a connection. Apparently there wasn't.

"What did you say to her?" Ryan's server stood in front of him with her hand on her hip.

"Pardon me?"

"You must have said something to Madison to get her to run off. What did you say?"

"I..." Ryan thought about his options and decided on honesty. "I asked her if she'd care to go out sometime."

"Out where? To the cemetery on a dark night? Serial killer pajama party?"

"Give him a break, Chloe!" The guy with the tool belt spoke up from his seat at the next counter. "The guy just got shot down."

"Dylan, don't you have a leaky sink to fix somewhere?"

"He asked if she wanted to go out for dinner or drinks. I don't think he was going to plunder and pillage her."

The server broke into a smile. "Is that all? What did she say?" Chloe turned her attention back to Ryan.

"She said, 'Thank you, but no.'"

"Are you joking?"

"This is a little embarrassing. I think I'll cut my losses and head out."

"Nonsense. She left anyway. I saw her drive off in her truck."

"She left?" Ryan's stomach sank. He didn't mean to run her off. This was awful.

"She has a meeting at the bank this afternoon, but you still have me." The server winked and held out her hand. "I'm Chloe."

He shook her hand firmly. "I'm Ryan. I think it's time for me to leave."

"You haven't even eaten yet. And we have fresh blueberry pie today if you're interested in dessert."

Ryan glanced over his shoulder at the parking lot as if he, too, would see Madison driving away. He eyed his plate with a walleye sandwich and fries. "I was looking forward to trying the pie."

"You won't be disappointed. Right, Dylan?"

"You can't go wrong with pie." Dylan agreed.

He stayed and ate his lunch. He couldn't resist and ordered that piece of pie, as well. Chloe wasn't kidding. Ryan enjoyed his sandwich, but the pie was incredible. It tasted like someone took a slice of summer and served it on a dessert plate.

The guy with the tool belt stood to leave. "Hey man. Don't let them give you a hard time around here. They're nice ladies underneath it all."

"Good to know. Thanks for sticking up for me."

"No trouble at all. See you around."

Chloe came around to settle Ryan's bill. "Aren't you glad you stayed?"

"I thought it would be weird, but I am glad. That pie is incredible. I still feel bad about running Madison off, though. I guess I went way off the mark with that one."

"No. You were spot on."

"I'm confused. She said no."

"Right. Madison is... complicated."

"Having dinner is complicated?"

Chloe grinned. "For some people."

Ryan settled his tab, which included another slice of pie, to go. His mind spun as he drove back to the lake home. Chloe had been too busy to chat much after telling him Madison was complicated. He did not need drama right now. There was enough to worry about already, starting with how many calls he missed by turning his phone off for lunch.

His mind drifted back to Madison. He couldn't deny his physical attraction to her. He wanted to release her honey blonde hair and run his fingers through her tresses. When she licked her lips, he wanted to kiss them, soft and slow.

But Ryan wanted more than a roll in the hay. He wanted to get to know Madison. She seemed young. How did she come to own a restaurant? What was her story? Why was he so drawn to her?

He pulled into the driveway of the rental home. A minivan was parked in front of the first garage door. Ryan pulled in next to it and wondered if it belonged to the cleaning service. They were supposed to come in the morning. He hoped they were almost finished so he could work in peace. He turned on his phone as he walked up the path and entered the lake house. Immediately, his phone buzzed with messages and voicemails.

"Bro! You want a sandwich?"

Ryan looked up from his phone and saw his brother standing in the kitchen. "Jake! No, I already ate." They hugged briefly. "When did you get in?"

"About 10 minutes ago. Beer?"

"Sure. Wait. You're driving a minivan?"

"Ha ha, yeah. I ordered a convertible, but they didn't have any available." Jack cracked the beer open before handing it over. "Dad's having Danica drive a Beemer here for me."

"Danica?"

"His latest personal assistant."

"What happened to Avery?"

"She married one of Dad's friends and is now a world-famous influencer."

Ryan shook his head. "Whatever that is."

"Dad said to put Danica in the room across from you."

"At least they aren't sleeping together."

"You can get in a lot of trouble for that, Bro!"

They exchanged a look. They knew their father had done it before, but it wasn't anything they condoned.

Physically, they looked like brothers. They were both tall, blond-haired and blue-eyed. The differences ended there. Ryan wore his hair slicked back, preferred polo shirts and khaki shorts, and had an appendix scar. Jake tousled his hair, and it almost fell into his eyes. He wore worn T-shirts and baggy shorts and had an arm tattoo of a wolf.

Their personalities were distinct, too. Ryan wondered if it's because Jake had lived mainly with their mother after their parents separated. Ryan had already graduated from high school and had started preparing for college during the divorce. He felt a lot of pressure to do the right thing, get the right degrees, and work hard like his father.

Jake earned good grades in school, but they came much more easily for him. He didn't have the pressure from their father. If he wanted to hang out with friends, no one was there to ask if they came from the right families or had the right connections.

They spent a few minutes catching up together over their beers before they went their separate ways. Ryan took his laptop out to the patio to get some work done. Jake headed to the basement to connect his gaming system and spend the afternoon with a controller in his hands. Several hours passed before they talked again.

"Hey, Ryan."

Ryan glanced up from the contract he was reviewing. "Hey."

"Are we doing anything for supper?"

Time passed by too quickly at the lake, especially when Ryan spent his time working. It was already after 7:00 pm. "I could grill some brats."

"Or," Jake smiled mischievously, "we could go out."

Ryan, stiff from sitting at the patio table all day, stood slowly. He stretched to get the kinks out. "Where do you want to go?"

"I found a few choices. The Corner bar and grill; Campers, a bar that serves frozen pizza; and the Sunflower Café, which sounds like a diner."

"The Sunflower is pretty good, but I ate there for lunch. Hard pass on the frozen pizza. Let's try The Corner."

"Cool. Are you planning on wearing that polo?" Jake eyed Ryan's outfit.

"Why? Did I spill something?"

"We're not in the city. We're not going to a country club. Don't you have a T-shirt to wear or something?"

Ryan dressed to impress every day. If he ran into a client outside of work, he wanted to appear professional. He couldn't remember the last time he wore a T-shirt. He thought maybe some time in college. Jake came to his rescue and brought him a shirt.

"What is a feather dream?"

Jake shook his head. "You're not that old, man. The Feather Dreams are a band. We'll listen to their playlist on the way."

It took some time to find the place. Ryan pulled up to a building that appeared to be an old factory or sawmill. It seemed as if a good wind would blow the whole place over. He wanted to throw the Escalade into reverse, but Jake jumped out and made his way to the door. Ryan was tempted to leave him there. He put the SUV in park and jumped out to join his brother.

The entryway light seemed low after the bright sunshine. A sign read "Open Seating" but finding a seat didn't seem to be a simple task. Ryan had hoped it wouldn't be busy, but the place was packed. They searched until they found a booth and slid in.

A frazzled server came over and took their drink orders. Despite all the people, she came back with their beers in a few minutes. They raised their mugs to each other before drinking. Jake grilled Ryan for a few minutes about how he liked the Feather Dreams' music. Ryan started in on how classic rock was better. They argued about who had to stay sober enough to drive home. Ryan had just lost the fight when he saw the server from the café come in. She scanned the crowd and smiled when she spotted him. She made her way over to their booth.

"Hey stranger!"

"Hello, Chloe."

"You remembered my name. Gold star for you today. Who's your handsome friend?"

Ryan introduced his brother.

"How old are you?" Chloe asked Jake.

Jake choked on his beer. He stared at Chloe, wondering if she was serious. He decided she was. "I'm twenty-two."

"Darn! Too young for me."

Jake kept his face straight. "You're breaking my heart, beautiful."

Chloe laughed and turned to Ryan. "Hey, scoot over. I've been on my feet all day. I want to sit."

Ryan moved to let her into the booth.

"I won't stay long. I was wondering…"

Ryan waited patiently for her to gather her thoughts.

She looked him square in the eye. "How long are you in town for?"

"Until Sunday."

"And then what?"

Understanding struck Ryan. "If everything works out to plan, I'll finish packing my house, put in my last week at work and I'll be moving out here."

Jake's jaw almost hit the floor.

Chloe didn't seem to notice. "You seem like a nice guy. I know talking to Madison didn't go so well today, but I have a good feeling about you. I have terrible luck with love, but I am good at spotting a match. Not that you're in love. Yet." She winked at Ryan.

"I don't think she's interested. She didn't even want to go out on a date."

A thin guy with brown curly hair and an angular face slid in next to Jake. "Hey, Chloe. Who are your friends?"

"Hey, Jesse, this is Ryan. He has a crush on our girl, Madison. And this is his brother, Jake. All I know about him is that he's too young for me."

Jesse raised an eyebrow at Jake. "Are we joining them or heading off to the bar?"

"Bar, there's a vodka cranberry over there with my name on it. Thanks for letting me sit with you guys for a minute. Nice to meet you, Jake!" With that, Chloe and Jesse slid off through the crowd.

Ryan regularly dealt with high pressure situations. He made a good living off complicated deals. But he wasn't sure he was ready to deal with the frown on Jake's face.

"Move here? Who's Madison? What?"

"Yes, move here. I have an opportunity to establish a winery and I'm taking it. I'm tired of the rat race, Jake. I need something different."

Jake chuckled, and Ryan relaxed. "That's awesome news! What the hell, though, a winery? Do you need overalls for that? Have you told dad yet?"

"Yes, a winery. I know it's a completely different direction, but the timing is right. It feels right. And no. I don't need overalls and I haven't told dad. Yet. It's on the agenda."

"That is not going to go well, man. Let me know if you want backup."

"I appreciate it."

"And Madison?" Jake didn't let her name slide.

"She owns the café. I asked her out, but she turned me down."

This time, Jake laughed out loud. "Are you serious? And this Chloe wants you to ask her out again? Bad idea."

"Definitely a bad idea." But Ryan knew he would.

CHAPTER 9

*D*ays off were marvelous. Madison tried to make the most of them. She didn't mind burying herself in her work, but she needed time to recharge. Tasks and chores still needed to get done. If she started early enough, she got everything finished by lunchtime. The rest of the day she would be free to do as she pleased. As always, she started with her least favorite task, cleaning the main house.

Madison didn't have any siblings. She had inherited everything when her parents died, including the hundred-year-old family lake house with a two-stall garage and tiny guest cabin. She had her mom's silver sedan and kept her dad's old red S-10. Down the road, between the gift shop and the laundromat, she had also inherited the Sunflower Café.

She couldn't face selling any of it. She also couldn't bring herself to live in the main house. Everything in there remained the same as the day her parents died. Her mom's reading glasses were still on the end table by her reading chair. Her father's purple and gold sweatshirt still lay across the back of a chair at the kitchen table.

Any time she entered the house, she expected her parents to greet her. Her mom should be arranging flowers, fixing iced tea, or baking something sweet. Her dad should be reading the paper, mowing the lawn, or tinkering with some house project. She cleaned it as fast as possible.

Madison had kept the restaurant. She drove her father's old red truck, and she had taken over her mother's fabulous flower gardens. It helped her feel like her parents were still a part of her life. The rest of it was too hard to deal with.

She sped through her chores and did a quick grocery shop. Chloe would pick her up at 12:30 and she had a lot of gardening to get through. Madison started with the potted flowers. Burying her face in each explosion of colors, she breathed in the scent of the blooms. She couldn't help herself. The fragrance of the flowers transported her away from it all. For a short time, she could forget about work. The pain of losing her parents faded away. The loneliness disappeared.

When she lifted her face into the sunshine, she had a smile of contentment on her face. Making sure the soil had enough moisture and safeguarding the plants from weeds didn't seem like work to Madison. The enchantment of the gardens was all the reward she needed.

She knelt in the dirt of a butterfly garden, pruning some spent pinks, when her phone rang. Disappointed to be pulled out of her musings, she set her trimmers aside and pulled off a gardening glove. She pulled her phone out of her back pocket. At least it was a cheerful call and not work.

"Grandma! How are you today?" Madison rocked back to sit on the grass. They made small talk for a few minutes until her grandpa wanted a turn to talk.

"Beautiful girl!"

"Hi, Grandpa!"

"I wanted to be sure you're all ready for tomorrow. Did you get a good rate at the bank?"

Madison assured her grandpa all was well, and that she wasn't worried. She had a substantial down payment, a good interest rate, and she knew Andy and Molly were offering a good deal. It had been a while since she had spoken to them, but they knew she wanted the property. The only thing left was to meet the realtor and sign on the dotted line. Nothing should go wrong.

Her grandma came back on the line to tell her they had to get their lunch ready. She wished Madison luck. They said their *I love you*s and said goodbye.

Madison checked the time on her phone and had a moment of panic. The clock read noon. She had a half hour to get ready. The dirt on her knees and the blades of grass in her hair had to go.

Pulling herself together took some rushing around. She managed to brush the grass out of her hair and clean off the streaks of dirt. She scrutinized her outfit. The little flowers on her cover-up matched the dusty rose bikini she wore. She had to dig in her closet for a few moments, but she found her water shoes in the back of the closet. She wheeled her cooler out to the driveway as Chloe pulled up in her bright yellow Jeep.

"Madison, darling, you look marvelous! It's nice to see you let your hair down!"

"Thanks Chloe, you look amazing, too. How did you find heart shaped sunglasses the same red as your bikini?"

"It was a thrift shop miracle!" Chloe hopped out of the Jeep to help Madison lift the cooler into the back. Pointing out her toes, she said, "My polish matches too!"

They didn't waste any time heading down the road. It took time to drive anywhere in lakes country. Everything was spread out.

When they arrived at the rental shop, most of their friends were already there, picking through the tubes and loading everything on the bus. The driver would take them a mile upriver, and they would float back to the rental shop. Madison put her phone in the glove box for Chloe to lock up. She tossed her cover-up in the back seat and went to the back of the Jeep to get her cooler.

"Here, let me do that!" Jesse, always the gentleman, grabbed the cooler and loaded it onto the bus for her.

Madison and Chloe signed their waivers and dug into the pile of tubes.

"Hey, girls!"

"Mindy! How did you get away from the kids?" Madison asked, happy to see her friend.

"Actually, Chloe ran into my mother-in-law at the grocery store and asked how the kids were doing. Then Chloe reminded her that summer was almost over and asked if she had spent enough time with the kids because school started soon. And wouldn't it be great if she could watch them so I could come tubing with all of you?"

"Chloe, you are something else." Madison studied her friend's sly smile. "I think your talents are wasted here. You should be negotiating world peace. Does anyone ever say no to you when you want something?"

"Nope. Everyone falls for my charm. But don't worry, I only use my powers for good!"

"Hey, if you can get me a child-free afternoon to spend time with other adults, I'm all for it. I love my kids, but sometimes I feel like I'm knee deep in crayons, robots, and princess parties. I miss you guys!"

"Yes! I miss this too." Madison grinned. "I didn't even realize how much. This is going to be great."

"You're both welcome!"

Madison and Mindy pulled Chloe into a hug.

Soon they were all on the bus. The ride filled with music and laughter. The driver dropped them off, and they all made a dash to the water. Someone played their summer playlist, filling the air with country music. People chatted, laughed, and splashed at each other while they floated along.

Madison lay back and enjoyed the sun on her face and the chatter of her friends. It felt strange. She spent her days making sure everyone else was happy. She couldn't even remember the last time she had relaxed for fun.

Her mind drifted back to her grandparents. *Now don't work too hard... Find someone to fancy, will you?...*

The Cloud Lake Resort would be a huge project. She needed to think through her plans. Her family and friends deserved to be a bigger priority in her life. There had to be a way to find a better balance. She stared up at the sky.

There were a few wisps of white clouds, and the sun blazed brightly. A soft breeze rustled the leaves of the trees along the bank. Madison trailed her hands in the cool water. She scooped up the water and let it run over her stomach. The small trails of water helped cut the heat. Her tube swirled as they floated. She listened to Mindy and Chloe chatting away, occasionally chiming in with her own comments. Mostly, she relaxed in her own little world.

Madison wasn't paying any attention to where her tube floated. She hit a patch of rapids too far to the side and her tube wedged into a pile of rocks. The water rushed by, and she couldn't push herself off. Her tube flipped over, dumping her into the water. She tried to stand up but fell into a river stone and yelped.

"Madison!" Chloe tried to get closer.

"I'm fine," Madison called out. She found her footing and pulled her tube off the rocks. "Oh, but my tube is not." It made an ominous hissing sound. She sloshed over to the shore, where the water ran slower. Chloe and Mindy stopped and fought the river to get back to her.

"Oh no, Madison! What should we do?" Mindy went into mom mode and checked Madison over. "Are you really okay?"

"Yes, really." Madison was more embarrassed than anything.

"Want to hop on with me?"

"Chloe! We can't both fit on a tube! Where are we?"

"I think we're by the golf course." Mindy inspected Madison's deflating tube.

"I definitely heard someone yell FORE!" Chloe raised an eyebrow. "Want me to help you hunt down some studs?"

Madison laughed. "I think I can manage. You girls catch up with the group. I'm going to flag down a golfer. Someone will have a cell phone I can use."

"Are you sure you're going to be okay?"

"Make sure to flash them some skin!"

"Thanks Mindy. I'll be fine. It's not that big of a golf course. And Chloe, if I show any more skin, I'll be arrested!"

Mindy and Chloe reluctantly left her to catch up with the rest of their friends.

Madison clambered her way through the trees flanking the river. She hoped she didn't add a bunch of scratches to the welts forming on her legs. She made it through to the manicured lawn of the golf course.

"Are you all right?"

Four golfers stared at her. She saw a tall, gorgeous, dark-haired woman; a stocky, older, lighter-haired man; a lanky blond who looked out of place in his faded gray shirt and baggy shorts; and Ryan – mister tall, tan, and handsome.

CHAPTER 10

Ryan was miserable. He hated golfing with his dad. Scott talked nonstop about business. He complained about the course and how it didn't compare to his usual courses. He harped on what the boys should do with their lives. His loud, commanding voice ranted nonstop.

He also drank too much. The more he drank, the more belligerent he became. He got mad at every little thing that didn't go his way.

Danika took it like a champ. She took notes and soothed Scott's temper. Her game stayed competitive. Ryan wondered how much his father paid her.

Jake didn't seem able to focus. The more their father ranted the more distracted he seemed to be. Usually, he was a decent golf partner, but his head wasn't in the game. It provoked more ranting and raving from Scott.

Ryan wanted it all to be over. He stared into the distance. A rustling in the trees caught his attention. Madison emerged like a vision. Her honey blonde hair blew in the breeze. Her pink bikini looked like a blush on her sun-kissed skin. Coming out of the band of trees she could have been mother nature herself. His eyes darkened. Digging deep he fought to restrain his primal attraction.

"Are you all right?" He looked her over. Every mark on her body caught his attention. He tried to avoid the fact she was practically naked, but it was impossible. He found her stunning.

"Not entirely. My tube is deflating. Do you have a phone? Or can I get a ride to the clubhouse? I need to get back to the tube shack."

"I have a phone, but you don't have to wait for a ride. I can drive you somewhere."

"Like hell, son. We're playing golf here. Call the clubhouse and have them send someone for her. We don't have to give up our afternoon for some girl."

Ryan froze for a moment. The whole afternoon, his father had been bellowing and barking orders. Ryan's nerves were shot.

"Dad, seriously? Let them take the cart and send one back for us." Jake wouldn't have it.

Ryan steeled himself and flashed his smile. "It's not a big deal, Dad. She needs help. We'll play golf some other time."

Danica spoke up. "Let them go, Scott. I'll call for the cart. They won't take long."

"Fine. We'll make it a twosome. Both of you boys can go." Scott glowered at his sons.

Jake shrugged and threw his bag in the back of the cart. "I rode with Ryan, anyway."

Madison and Ryan took the seats in the front. Jake climbed into the back. Ryan didn't waste time heading to the clubhouse. If his dad changed his mind, he didn't want to listen to any more yelling.

"Sorry about that, Madison. My dad forgets he's a human being like the rest of us." Ryan lost his confident, calm voice and sounded small and quiet.

Madison put a hand on his arm. "I'm sorry I disturbed his afternoon, but I appreciate your help."

He glanced over at her. He didn't understand it, but he would capture the sun if she asked him to. "We were in the right place at the right time. There aren't many golfers out this afternoon."

Jake held the tube in the backseat with him. "You snagged a fishhook."

Madison turned to look at him. "A fishhook? Really?"

He showed her the rusty hook. "Really."

"I wonder where it came from. No one fishes in the tubing stretch."

Ryan stole another look at her. "I'm glad it hooked the tube and not you."

Madison sighed, "That's true. I'm disappointed I had to bail on my friends though."

Jake seemed to wake up at the mention of Madison's friends. "Were Chloe and Jesse there?"

"You know Chloe and Jesse?"

"We met them last night," Jake explained.

"We were at The Corner," Ryan added.

Madison smiled. "That doesn't surprise me. The Corner is Chloe's home away from home. She still lives with her parents and her brothers drive her crazy. She is currently without a boyfriend, so she wrangles Jesse into going with her."

"Jesse isn't dating anyone?" Jake asked.

"Nope. He's free as a bird." Madison replied.

They returned the golf cart and made sure someone planned to bring one out to Scott and Danica. The staff assured them a cart was already on the way. They all piled into Ryan's Escalade.

"Where to?"

"Take a left. It's just up the road. There's a large purple sign."

It wasn't far to the tube shack, but Ryan was glad he could drive Madison. He didn't like the thought of her walking back alone, wearing a bikini and sunglasses. As soon as he parked, Madison jumped out of the car.

"Thanks for the ride."

Ryan didn't want to let her go. "We can wait with you."

"You don't have to. I'll be fine here."

Jake jumped out of the car. "We don't mind. We'll wait until your friends come back. It won't be much fun to sit by yourself."

Madison suddenly seemed self-conscious. She grabbed her wrap out of the back seat of a Jeep. She turned away from them as she pulled it on.

"Company sounds nice. I appreciate it. Give me a minute." Madison went to turn in her tube.

Ryan couldn't help himself and watched her walk away. Even covered with the wrap, her body excited him. She was gorgeous. It wasn't the clothes or lack of them. It was the way she carried herself. She was self-assured, but feminine. She was strong and soft at the same time. Madison intrigued him more than any woman had before.

Jake noticed him watching her. "She's so normal. I'm pleasantly surprised with you."

"You're forgetting she turned me down."

"She's letting us hang out with her now."

"Maybe she's being nice because we helped her out."

"Maybe." Jake gave him a look that said he didn't think that was the reason.

Ryan glared at Jake. "Thanks for the encouragement."

Jake laughed.

Madison returned carrying slips of paper. "They gave me a refund and two vouchers to tube for free."

"People seem nice around here," Ryan said.

"They are. Do either of you want them? I don't have time to come back. This was sort of a one-time deal for me."

The brothers eyed each other.

"I can give them to Chloe if you can't use them."

Jake spoke first. "We'll take them."

Ryan watched Madison hand them over. He wondered what his brother planned to do with them. Ryan didn't have any more time to go tubing than Madison did.

"Does the restaurant keep you that busy?" Ryan asked Madison.

"It's pretty time-consuming."

"I can understand that," Ryan said. "I've been working more than I've been relaxing on this trip."

"Not me. The media room is incredible. I love gaming in there."

"Are you guys staying at the Carter house?" Madison asked.

"How did you guess?" Ryan grinned at her.

"None of the other cabins at the Cloud Lake Resort have media rooms." She smiled.

Ryan grimaced.

Madison laughed at his expression. "It's not a bad thing. It's a magnificent house."

"You've been in it before?" Jake asked.

"Sure," Madison said. "For work. We catered a few parties for the Carters before they decided to rent the place out."

"Cool. Hey Ryan, let's throw a gigantic party. We can see how many relatives we can fit in the hot tub."

"Hard pass on that one, Jake. No, thank you."

Madison laughed. "I can see Andy and Molly in their bathing suits telling your cousins to scoot over and make room."

"I wonder how many kegs we would need?" Jake asked.

"Probably a lot if I know your cousins. I think Camille and Patricia prefer mixed drinks." Madison grinned. "It's been a few years since we've hung out, but your cousins sure threw some wild parties."

"When we visited, I was too young to party. After our parents divorced, I hardly saw them." Jake said. "How about you, Ryan?"

"No, Dad hated coming here. He'd be miserable and make Mom miserable. She would give up and we'd go home."

"Dad sure puts the fun in dysfunctional," Jake said with a laugh.

Ryan's smile turned wry. "Do you know them pretty well? Our cousins?"

Madison tilted her head while she thought. "Yes and no. Our high school was pretty small and we all kind of hung out with everyone. We ended up at a lot of summer bonfires together, but we weren't close friends.

"Actually, that's not entirely true. One of my favorite summer memories is with Camille and Patricia. One of our parties broke up and I couldn't find my ride. They brought me back to the resort. We made Aaron and Manny go out and bring us the swimming raft. We floated out on the lake watching the stars. The night sky had so many shooting stars we lost count. We laid out there until the sun rose. Andy found us fast asleep floating in the middle of the lake."

Jake thought for a moment, "At my favorite high school party we played some old cartridge video games and ate purple pancakes."

"Purple pancakes?" asked Madison.

"We only had blue and red food coloring. Otherwise, they probably would have been brown."

Madison laughed. "That sounds like fun, too."

"Hello Madison, Ryan, Jake."

"Hey Jesse, where's Chloe?" Madison asked.

"She's not far behind. I'm done with the sun. I needed shade."

"Madison! You're alive! You have TWO knights in shining armor!" Chloe ran up to hug Madison.

"They are two golfers, not knights, but they did rescue me." Madison smiled at Ryan.

"We have to reward their bravery. Let's take them out for pizza and nachos."

The guys eyed each other.

"Oh, I'm sure they don't want..." Madison started.

"Sounds good!" Jake broke in before she could protest further.

"But your dad. Don't you want to get back to him?"

Jake laughed. "Danica can take care of him."

Ryan gave his brother a look and let out a breath. "It's happy hour. He's a few fingers into his bourbon by now, and he's been drinking all afternoon on the course. He won't cool off until tomorrow. Where are we going? The Corner?"

"I'm out. I have to get home to the kids. Stay out of trouble." Mindy gave out a round of goodbye hugs.

"I'm in. I need nachos. Who can I ride with? Mindy picked me up." Jesse chimed in.

"You can ride with us." Ryan said. "We have plenty of room. Right, bro?" He raised an eyebrow at his brother.

"I need to change first." Embarrassment made Madison's cheeks rosy. "I'm not going to the bar in a bikini and a cover-up. Chloe, let's stop by my place on the way and find something to wear."

"You got it, boss."

CHAPTER 11

Chloe dug through Madison's closet looking for a sundress. "If I'd known you would run into Ryan and Jake, I would have popped your tube myself."

"Gee, thanks. What would I ever do without good friends like you?"

"I want the red one. It will fit my chest and match my sunglasses." Chloe pulled out a strapless red floral sundress with a stretchy tube top. She popped into the bathroom to change. "And I am, you know, the best of friends. I want you to be happy, Madison!"

"I know. I know. Thanks, Chloe." Madison picked out a flowing, soft pink sundress. "I guess if we're sticking to color themes." She held the dress out and examined it. The skirt seemed a little shorter than she liked, and the top a little lower than she usually wore.

Chloe came out of the bathroom looking like a starlet. She glanced over at Madison. "It's perfect. I love how the top will make a bow in the back. Super cute."

"Maybe I should find something else."

"Mm, no. That's the one. What's wrong with it?"

"Nothing. I don't want to give Ryan the wrong idea."

"What, that you're gorgeous and wear pink dresses?"

Madison laughed. "You're right. I'm being silly. I'll change and we can be on our way."

Cars packed the parking lot when they pulled up to The Corner. Madison had butterflies in her stomach. She wished she had worn something else. Jean shorts and a tank top would be more comfortable, and she forgot to bring a sweater. What if the evening cooled off?

She had to work early in the morning. She wouldn't be able to drink very much, or tomorrow would be miserable. If everyone came, they would never find a table big enough for them all. Ordering food would take forever with all the people.

"Are you going to sit in the Jeep all night?" Chloe practically hopped up and down in anticipation. She was always bursting with energy.

Madison shook off her nerves and climbed out of the Jeep. She concentrated on the sound of the gravel crunching under her sandals. Her mind wandered to Ryan. He had been so thoughtful. It was easy to talk to him and his brother, but those eyes of his drew her in every time.

The girls made their way into the bar and pushed through the crowd. It didn't take long to find everyone. Almost the entire group from tubing had come and then some. Those who missed out on the afternoon fun had come to enjoy the evening with them. They had an entire section of the bar to themselves.

The only spots left were at a table with Ryan, Jake, and Jesse. They had crammed together on half the table to leave the other half for Madison and Chloe.

Sitting next to Jesse, Chloe started laughing. "Guys, you can spread out. We're not giants."

Madison sat and watched Ryan move his chair closer to hers. He took more space, but not enough to make her uncomfortable. It reminded Madison of her parents. They always left a little room, but sat close enough to share a soft-spoken joke, hold hands, or even kiss.

"We ordered some pizza, nachos, and pitchers of beer for everybody. If you want something else though, add it to our tab."

"Vodka cranberry for me!" Chloe would settle for seltzer on the river, but otherwise, her drink of choice was vodka with cranberry juice.

Madison thought for a moment. She didn't drink often. She didn't enjoy running the restaurant after a crazy night out. But she'd enjoyed the day and had sparkling water along with her hard seltzers. She was careful to drink moderately.

"Would you care to share a bottle of wine?"

She smiled at Ryan. "I've been here a million times and they've never had wine, much less bottles of them."

"They do. I brought them a half a case this morning. The owner opened one for the staff to try tonight and I think he wants to bring one home for dinner on Sunday, but I'm sure there are a few bottles left."

"I'd love a glass of wine. Why would you bring them wine?"

"I wanted to see what they thought of it."

"Do you sell wine? Are you a distributor or something?"

"Nothing like that. I actually made it. I have a dream to own my own winery. I've been testing different grape varieties."

Madison looked over at Chloe to see if she had heard what Ryan was saying, but Chloe was chatting with Jake and Jesse. They were talking about some video game everyone played.

Ryan explained. Commercial real estate wasn't his passion. He had plenty of money and it wasn't making him any happier. The intense pressure to perform and close deals was getting to him. He wanted to leave it all and start a winery.

"We don't have any wine glasses. Are these okay?" The server had some plastic cups on her tray.

Ryan nodded and she set them on the table. Chloe, Jake, and Jesse took their drinks and went off to play arcade games. Madison and Ryan stayed behind to drink their wine. Ryan poured her a glass before he poured one for himself. Madison noticed and appreciated the consideration.

Madison had taken Wine Tasting 101 in college. Her friend had talked her into it after they discovered the class offered a credit. She tried to remember what to do. She sniffed the bouquet, swirled the glass to see the legs, and took a small sip to taste it. She could pick out a raspberry flavor and a light touch of chocolate and oak.

"This is really nice. I feel weird drinking wine and eating pizza though."

"If you can't drink it with pizza, is it even worth drinking?"

Madison laughed. "I do love pizza." She helped herself to another slice. "Tell me more, why a winery?"

"It all started when I was in college. I was heading to my mom's place for Christmas and hadn't gotten her anything. I didn't want to show up empty handed so I picked up a case of expensive wine. She was excited to try it and opened a bottle for dinner. It was awful. I felt terrible. We joked about it during dinner and my mom said something about how I could have made better wine."

Madison nodded, listening intently.

Ryan continued, "I thought it would be hilarious to make my mom some wine. I did some quick research, ordered what I needed and got to work. The next Christmas I showed up with a case of the wine I made. Again, my mom opened it for dinner. This time the wine was excellent. When she found out I had made it she insisted I make more. I've enjoyed making it ever since. As for opening a winery here, Napa is too crowded. Doing it here makes more sense."

"I didn't even know you could grow grapes here."

"Absolutely, you can. So, what about you? What are your dreams in life, Madison?"

"Hmm. I'm not so sure anymore." Madison paused for a moment and sipped her wine. She thought about tomorrow when she would meet with the realtor to buy the resort. She wasn't comfortable spilling everything out to a practical stranger, but he had been so open about his own dreams. "Honestly," she gave in and shared, too, "I love the restaurant. It means so much to me. I have plans for expanding the business."

"But?"

"I used to have different dreams. Like a lot of my friends, I wanted to move away after college. They live in these city lofts, or have these fabulous careers, or drive fancy cars, or dine in amazing restaurants. I thought I wanted those things too."

"And now?"

"Now I have my little cottage and it feels like it's enough. I have a successful country café. I drive my dad's old pickup. I've learned how to cook. I have wonderful friends. I'm thriving and I want our community to thrive too."

Ryan held her gaze for a moment. "Do you want to get out of here?"

Madison didn't even try to fight it. "Yes. Yes, I do."

They made sure Jake and Jesse had rides home and said goodbye to their friends. Chloe winked at Madison on the sly and murmured, "Text me later. And get 'em tiger." Madison knew her face flushed as red as the dress Chloe had worn. She wouldn't sleep with him. It had been a long day, and Madison didn't want to stay out too late. Ryan procured another bottle of wine on their way out the door and promised the owner he'd replace what he had taken.

They climbed into Ryan's SUV. "Where to?"

Madison hesitated. Second thoughts crept into her mind. Madison tried to think of a nice way to put it.

"Would you rather just have a ride home? You've had a long day."

"It's probably best. I have to work early tomorrow and it's going to be a busy day."

"Are you comfortable with me driving or should I go get Chloe?"

"Oh no. If you don't mind. I'd appreciate it if you drove me home. I trust you. Chloe has your brother, after all. If I don't text her I'm all right, she'll hold him hostage for me."

Ryan laughed. "I'd hate to see what Chloe could do to him. I'll get you home safe and sound."

They drove in silence for a few minutes.

"May I ask a question?"

Madison turned a little in her seat to face him better. She knew what was coming. "Sure."

"How did you end up with the restaurant?"

The question never got easier. "The short answer is my parents died in a boating accident and I inherited it."

"I'm so sorry!"

"It was devastating, and I guess I never really took time to grieve. I couldn't face selling the place. I started running it and now here I am."

"How long has it been?"

"Four years."

"I'm so sorry. Damn, I already said that. I don't know what to say."

"No one does. I know you mean well. What about you? What's your family like?" Madison was eager to change the subject.

"Well, you've met my dad. He's a hard man who's had more than his fair share of success." Ryan thought about it a moment. "No. He's an asshole. He always has been and probably always will be. My mom, Laura, is the complete opposite. She's kind and caring and much better off. Then there's my brother, the boy wonder. And me."

"Oh, the turn is coming up. By that yellow mailbox."

Ryan slowed and turned into her driveway. "This is your house?" In front of him stood a beautiful old house. There were pillars and an old-fashioned veranda. A few of the front windows had stunning stained glass in them. A sea of flowers and a perfectly manicured lawn surrounded the house.

"Yes, but..."

"You take care of all of this? And run a restaurant? And you're expanding?"

"Yes, but I don't stay in the house. I live in the guest cabin. There to the side."

"This was your parents' house."

"Yep."

"I'm being a bit of a jerk."

"No, you're not. You didn't know."

"You're being too nice to me."

"Maybe I am. Would you like to come in anyway?" Madison surprised herself. She had planned on saying goodbye. She wanted to get ready for bed after her long day, but she didn't want to be alone.

"I would."

The cabin was small and didn't have much room for furnishings. Madison's wrought iron bed fit into the front corner. A well-worn quilt with different colors of flower fabrics covered her bed. The two armchairs on the other side of the room were also wild with flowers. The back of the cabin held a tiny kitchenette on one side and a three-quarter bath on the other.

The intense intimacy overwhelmed Madison. She needed space. "Let's sit out back. We can watch the fireflies."

Madison led Ryan out the back door to the patio. The patio seemed large compared to the cabin. Wicker chairs and a set of lounge chairs offered comfortable seating choices. They were arranged around a pretty fire table. Madison turned the fire on low and asked Ryan to light the citronella candles scattered around on the side tables. She disappeared into the house. When she came back, she had blankets and a tray with iced teas and summer berries.

She set the tray on a table between the lounge chairs and offered Ryan a blanket. "If we lie here, maybe we can catch a shooting star, too."

Fireflies began twinkling in the yard. "I've never seen so many fireflies before. With all of your flowers and the lake, it's magical back here."

Madison smiled at him. "It's my happy place. My little slice of heaven on earth."

"I need a place like this. A place to relax after a hard day's work. That's what I've been missing."

"What's your place like?"

"It's ideal – an architectural masterpiece, in a great neighborhood, inspired decorating, immaculate landscaping – it's the perfect house. But it's not a home."

"I understand. I thought I wanted all of that. Sometimes I get jealous of my old friends who are living in those kinds of homes. I've been so driven I haven't stopped to think, but I'm realizing the life I have is pretty wonderful."

Madison knew she should ask Ryan to leave, but they kept talking in soft voices. The candles burned lower until they put themselves out. Madison and Ryan didn't notice. They had fallen asleep surrounded by the sounds of crickets and rustling leaves.

CHAPTER 12

The sun hadn't risen yet, but the dark had started to fade. Ryan rubbed his eyes and yawned before he remembered where he was. He turned to see Madison watching him with sleepy eyes.

With her blanket wrapped around her, she rose and came over to him. Her hair hung wild and free around her face. She took his hand, and he rose to stand. She put her free hand to the side of his face, and he gazed at her with a deep intensity. They drew closer to each other. Their lips came together as the sun's first rays glowed on the water. The soft start of the sunrise seemed to reflect the growing fires inside them.

Soft and slow, they kissed. Her sleepy, succulent, satisfying kisses warmed him in the cool morning air. The heady perfume of the flowers and the soft light made the moment seem even more surreal. Ryan wanted to savor the moment, but he also wanted more. He was hungry for her.

Madison, with a light touch, pushed him away and smiled sweetly. "Now get out. I have to get ready for work."

Ryan smiled back at her. "Dinner tonight?"

"I'll be working late."

"You're worth waiting for."

Feeling ecstatic, Ryan drove home. He didn't restrain himself. His smile was broad and goofy, and he didn't care. He allowed himself to enjoy this happiness, to replay their kiss over and over in his mind. His grin could last all day and he wouldn't bother to hide it.

Getting Madison to open up would take effort, but he looked forward to it. Especially if learning about her came with such sweetness. Something special about her set her apart from the women he normally dated. Yes, she was smart and successful, but she didn't wear her accomplishments like a badge. She worked hard and was more a part of the team than their boss. She seemed to enjoy her work for what it was and not what it could provide her. Those little contrasts made all the difference in the world to him.

As he walked to the front door, a car pulled into the drive. Jake climbed out wearing yesterday's clothes.

"Good morning."

"Morning, bro."

"Jesse?"

Jake nodded his head in agreement. "Madison?"

Ryan nodded his head as well.

They never talked about personal matters like relationships. Ryan knew his brother was gay, and Jake knew Ryan was straight. It was something they knew about each other, like how Ryan preferred podcasts and Jake liked rock music. Ryan couldn't even guess if Jake and Jesse had played video games or bedroom games all night. Ryan wondered if it would be weird to ask him. He turned towards his brother, but the front door swung open.

"Boys."

Ryan almost jumped out of his skin. "You startled me. Good morning dad."

"How do you always know when we get home?" Jake asked.

"Danica heard the car doors. She's making coffee and frying bacon. Let's have breakfast."

The brothers looked at each other and grinned.

"Sounds good." Ryan answered, and they followed Scott into the house.

"Smells outstanding, Danica." Jake followed his nose to the breakfast bar in the kitchen, and Ryan wasn't far behind.

Danica handed over steaming cups of coffee. "The quiche and bacon are almost done. Help yourself to berries while I finish cooking."

Ryan sipped his coffee and stole a glance at Danica. She was already put together and looked amazing. She wore makeup, styled her hair, and her outfit was immaculate. He thought of Madison with her hair wild in her rumpled pink sundress, so beautiful in the light of the rising sun. The difference struck a chord.

He hoped for another chance to see Madison looking wild and free. He couldn't stop thinking about their time together. It had been an unfamiliar experience for him. He'd never been able to talk to someone so easily and so late into the night. He had never slept under the stars and had never seen a woman so comfortable with herself in the morning. His last girlfriend always dashed into the shower as soon as she woke up. Like Danica, she didn't leave the bedroom for breakfast until she was all put together.

He looked forward to leaving his old life behind him. He wanted a new, more organic type of life, similar to those who lived at Cloud Lake. Where people waved when they drove past and opened doors for each other. Where people who didn't even know you took you into their circle as if you had always belonged there. Where being yourself was good enough.

Scott peered over his tablet. "Dammit, boys, did you see this? S&P dropped 1.6%. The economy is going to hell. The president better get his head out of the clouds if he wants to get reelected."

Danica cut into the quiche and began serving it. "It's a dip. There's nothing to bluster over. Earnings are going to outpace predictions for the quarter. Watch and see."

Jake stopped with his fork almost to his open mouth. Ryan steeled himself, waiting for his dad to explode.

"Watch and see, she says. Too smart for her own damn good." Scott grumbled and went back to reading the news.

The guys remained frozen. They had seen their fair share of personal assistants let go for much less than talking back to their father. Even when they disagreed with him themselves, they had to approach the situations politically and politely. And often still received an earful for it.

Danica saw them. "What? Is the quiche all right?"

Jake finished taking his bite. She settled her gaze on Ryan.

"The quiche is great. We're waiting for dad to say something. Usually, he explodes when someone disagrees with him." He didn't add "they usually get fired" to the end of his statement.

"I'm not a damn ogre."

"We have an understanding." Danica said. "He's the mental brains and I'm the mental brawn. That's why he hired me. I'm not afraid to redirect the conversation to better fit the situation."

"He hired you to redirect the conversation?" Ryan parroted what she said.

"Fucking fantastic." Jake laughed and earned a stern look from their father.

Scott cleared his throat. "The board may have mentioned I need to tone down some." Scott put his tablet on the counter. "What's on the agenda today? We can go fishing, try another game of golf or day drink in the boat."

"I need a few hours of sleep before I do anything." Jake said and yawned as if to prove his point. "I'll join you guys at lunch."

"I have some work to catch up on this morning, and I'm heading over to the resort this afternoon. I'm free for lunch, though," Ryan said.

His father held his tongue, but Ryan could see the upset on his dad's face. Scott's eyes squinted slightly, and his chin was jutting out. Ryan could read the subtle clues of his dad's annoyance, but he didn't understand where it was coming from. They didn't spend a lot of time together. Even when they took family vacations, they spent more time apart than they did with each other.

Finally, Scott's shoulders lowered, and he said, "Lunch with my boys then. We'll see you two around noon." He glanced over at Danica. "How about a round of golf?"

Jake left to crawl into his bed. Ryan walked towards his own wing. As he entered the hallway, he heard Danica counter with a flea market and an art walk. His dad seemed to have met his match.

Ryan took his time in the shower. The hot water relaxed his stiff muscles. He wouldn't trade the night for anything, but sleeping on a lounge chair in the cool night air had been rough on him. He wanted to remember the smells of this morning, the flowers, fresh air, faint smoke and the sweet strawberry of Madison's hair. His own body wash hinted at vanilla with bergamot and cedar, and it seemed to enhance his memory of their kiss.

He stepped out of the shower and dried himself off. The condensation clouding the mirror needed to be wiped off before he could start his morning routine. He grabbed his hair cream to slick his hair back, but he stopped. The hair cream went back on the counter.

He shook out his hair and ran his fingers through it to get it out of his eyes. Carefully, he studied his reflection. He would never pull off the casual look Jake wore, but he could live without the slicked back style.

Ryan dressed and considered his options. He could work in his room at the desk, or he could work on the deck again. He ran the risk of interruptions if he sat on the deck, but it also had sunshine, loons swimming by, and the sound of small waves hitting the shore. The deck won out.

He went into the kitchen to get an iced tea. Dad and Danica had already left. The house was quiet. He went outside and made himself comfortable. He turned on his laptop and read through his first email.

Ryan – I didn't want to call you while you are visiting Cloud Lake with your father. Are you moving? I ran into Sharon at the club. She said she stopped by your house to leave the information for the charity run you were interested in. She said your house is full of boxes. What on earth is going on? Call me! XOXO Laura Covington.

The email from his mom rubbed him the wrong way. For one, Ryan wasn't interested in the 5K. Sharon had caught him on one of his morning runs and had tried to talk him into it. Most of the people who attended her 5K charity runs were neighborhood stay-at-home parents. She tried to get him to attend so the other men of the neighborhood would take note and attend as well. Second, his boxes weren't anywhere near the front door, and he wondered what windows she had looked in to see them. He would have to check his security cameras to see what she had been doing. Third, he wasn't ready to tell people about his plans. How did she always know what he was up to?

Mom – I'll call you this evening. Love, Ryan

Ryan felt guilty about sneaking around. He preferred to keep his plans close to his chest, including his current plans. He didn't want to hurt anyone, but he didn't trust anyone either. The best way to break free from his old life was to sign on that dotted line and move forward. He didn't want to give anyone the chance to talk him out of his dreams.

He had researched as much as possible. He'd worked out his finances to secure a comfortable future. Even if everything completely failed, money wouldn't be a problem. He may not drive a brand-new Escalade if he failed to get the winery going, but he could certainly afford a secondhand sedan. He might fail. It took a minimum of three years to grow decent grapes. If your harvest went well, it could take several more years for fermenting and aging the wine. It could be longer than seven years before he saw profitability.

Running an actual farm worried him. Owning a winery didn't mean sitting around drinking wine and smoking cigars. It meant hard work, long days and fighting the elements. There were challenges ahead he couldn't even imagine. He'd prepared as much as possible for the unknown. The challenge excited him.

Right now, he had a different challenge. His inbox had way too many emails, and his daydreams needed to be set aside. He stood to stretch and walked around the deck. The loons were floating nearby, and he allowed himself a few minutes to watch them. He glanced at his watch. The morning had gotten away from him. He went back to his seat and buried himself in his work.

CHAPTER 13

Madison closed her eyes, pinched the bridge of her nose, and counted backwards from ten. When she opened her eyes, Chloe still stood in front of her with her hands on her hips, waiting for an answer.

"Yes."

"I knew it! He kissed you!"

"Chloe! You don't have to announce it to the entire world."

Chloe went into the hallway outside of the office. In exaggerated motions she looked to her left and then to her right. She came back in and plopped into the chair. "No one is around to hear. Benny and the kitchen crew are jamming out to some country music. The waitstaff are up front taking care of customers."

"Which is where we should be."

"Lunch rush hasn't even started and as your best friend I'm entitled to any and all details."

"That's not how it works. As your best friend, I'm entitled to privacy and can tell you to buzz off."

"Okay, fine. I'll just make up what happened in my head. 'Madison, you're so lovely, I need to kiss your lips.' This is where you gasp and place your hand on your chest. 'Why, I never! You're an out-of-towner. I wouldn't dream of it.' His eyes are smoldering at this point."

"Wait. Am I a Southern belle in this scenario? No one says, 'Why, I never,' Chloe. You're being ridiculous. Besides, I. Kissed. Him."

Chloe looked like the cat who caught the cream.

"Yes, I said it. I kissed him as the sun rose over the lake. The moment holds the title of most romantic moment of my life."

"As the sun rose?" Chloe sat up straighter in her chair. "He spent the night? In your bed?"

"No! We were out on the loungers by the fire table. We talked so late into the night we fell asleep. I woke as the sky lightened and he looked so handsome lying there with his hair ruffling in the breeze. He woke up and gazed at me and I think I lost my mind."

"Madison, that is so romantic. Are you going to see him again?"

"Tonight, after work. I told him I'd be late. And get this. He said, 'You're worth waiting for' before he left."

"Seriously?"

They both sighed at the same time.

"Seriously, we need to get to work."

"All right, fine, but the next tall, tan, and handsome to come in is all mine."

"Did someone say tall, dark, and handsome?" Benny walked into the office with a plate of fries.

"No way. Not in a million years, Benny." Chloe rolled her eyes.

He wiggled his eyebrows at her. "You can't do better than a chef, *mon chér.*"

"I could and I plan to." Chloe laughed. "Chef? Try café cook."

"You wound me deeply. For that I will share no jokes with you."

"Is that all it takes? I should have tried that years ago."

"Ouch, Chloe. Why so mean?"

"Sorry, Benny-boo. Forgive me?"

"Always."

"Good." Chloe stole one of Benny's french fries and practically skipped out of the office.

"Boss, we have a fry thief on our hands."

Madison walked over to him and stole one, too. "Two fry thieves."

"Are you going to skip out of here Chloe style?"

"Nope. I'm too old to skip. People would talk. What can I do for you, Benny?"

Benny scuffed a sneaker on the tile floor. "I'm wondering about Landon. I know you were off yesterday, but he's been texting me nonstop asking me if I've heard anything."

"I received a call back from his reference before Chloe came in here. The plan is to give him a shot on a trial basis. I'll call him after lunch, but you can let him know if you want."

"Thanks, Madison. He'll be great. You won't be disappointed."

"Good to hear."

Madison stole another fry from Benny before leaving the office. She arrived at the host stand in time to help Dusty with the lunch crowd. Madison did the greeting and Dusty did the seating. When there was a lull, Dusty grabbed the menus and Madison wiped them with disinfectant for the next group to use.

She enjoyed the busywork. It helped keep her mind off of her afternoon appointment. It was finally here. The day she would purchase the resort. Except every time she thought about it, her nerves spun out of control. Self-doubt filled her thoughts. She wished her parents were there to guide her. She tried to think of what they would say to her, but her mind blanked out.

"Are you okay?" Dusty handed her a stack of menus.

Madison set the menus on the counter. She didn't know how to answer. "I think so. Do you mind if I go grab a soda?"

"I can handle the host stand." Dusty assured her.

"Thanks," Madison seemed to squeak. She filled a glass with ice and soda and headed to her office. Sitting at her desk, she tried to compose herself. She took deep, even breaths to calm herself and her racing heart. Sipping her soda to settle her nerves, she picked up the picture of her parents.

"Am I doing the right thing?" she asked the picture.

"You always do the right thing, Madison," Chloe said softly from the doorway. "Are you getting cold feet?"

"Not exactly. All of a sudden, the feelings in my heart overwhelmed me. It's not just owning the resort. It's leaving this place behind."

"Sometimes you have to leave important things behind so you can move forward. And we're not going anywhere. The restaurant will be here anytime you need it. Anytime you need us."

"These last four years, I don't know if I could have done it without you and Benny and everyone else."

"You could have, but you didn't have to. And you won't be alone moving forward. We're here for you."

Madison smiled at Chloe. "You're a wonderful friend, Chloe. Thanks for the pep talk."

"Anytime boss. Now brace yourself. Tall, tan, and handsome and his group are here sitting by the windows. Can you handle a visit, or should I cover for you?"

"Ryan? His group?"

"Ryan, Jake, an older man, and a dark-haired woman who is absolutely stunning."

"His father and his father's personal assistant."

"Is that what they call her?" Chloe crinkled her nose.

Madison giggled. "I think her name is Danica, but I can ask them."

Chloe put an arm around Madison and gave her a squish before they left the office. "Today is your day, my friend. Go get 'em tiger."

"I will not roar."

"You totally should. You would feel amazing."

"No. Not happening."

"You're missing out." Chloe headed over to a customer who was flagging her down.

Madison realized she still had the picture of her parents in her hand and set it on the host stand on her way to Ryan's table. They all sat admiring the water. "Hello there."

Ryan smiled. "Dad, you remember Madison from yesterday. Madison, this is my dad, Scott, and his assistant, Danica."

"Hey, Madison," Jake greeted her with a smile as well.

Scott scrutinized Madison before reaching out a beefy hand. "Nice to meet you, Madison."

Danica gave Scott a look out of the side of her eye before she too reached out her hand. "It's a pleasure Madison. This is your café? You're so young."

Madison tried not to blush. "Yes. The Sunflower Café has been mine for about four years now. It was my dad's before, and I practically grew up in this place."

"Are you able to join us?" Ryan asked, trying to head off any more questions.

A cloud passed over Scott's face.

"I'd love to, but I can't. It's pretty busy today and I have to run for an appointment soon. I need to make sure everything is running smoothly before I go." Madison tried to ignore the darkening stare Ryan's father gave her. "Can I get you anything while I'm here?"

"I could use another coffee if you have the time. I'd prefer a bourbon, but apparently that's out of the question in your little café."

Ryan gave his dad a look before smiling thinly. "Dad, it's a café, not a bar."

"I'll make sure the pot is fresh. I'll be right back." Madison tried to walk tall but scurried away quickly. She didn't make it out of earshot before she heard Scott's voice.

"What do you think you're doing with that girl?"

She didn't wait to hear the answer.

A fresh pot of coffee was already brewing when she stepped into the wait station. She didn't have to wait long for fresh coffee, but she couldn't deny she needed another moment to calm herself. Ryan was so nice, but his dad seemed awful. She stood with her arms crossed, waiting for the last drips to finish.

"You going to make the rounds with that coffee or glare at it all afternoon?"

Madison glanced over at the counter. "Hey, Dylan. It's almost done. Need a refill?"

"Always."

"Another rough night?"

"I thought babies were supposed to sleep a lot. I think mine's defective." Dylan held out his cup for Madison.

"I'm not sure, but I hear it gets better." She poured in the steaming coffee.

"That's what they say."

Madison moved down the counter and filled a few more cups. She squared her shoulders and went over to Ryan's table.

"Here we are, fresh made."

Scott grunted as a reply.

"Thanks, Madison," Ryan said, looking her straight in the eye.

Whatever had happened at the table seemed to have settled. Ryan didn't seem ruffled by it, and his father seemed subdued. Madison wasn't sure if that was a good thing or not.

"You're welcome," she said with a wink at Ryan.

Before any more drama started, she headed over to the fishermen's table.

"Coffee, fellas?"

They all held out their cups for her.

"Any fish tales today?"

"Another handful of sunfish," Frank answered. "We'll need a barrel of breadcrumbs when we bread them for a fish fry."

"We don't have that many," Lenny said. "The freezer has all kinds of room in it for more fish."

"You've got to use cornmeal, not breadcrumbs," Ted said. "It makes a better batter."

"I've used breadcrumbs before. They work fine," Frank replied.

Ted eyed Madison. "What would you use?"

"I have to be honest with you. I'd use cornmeal. It seems to fry up better."

Ted could barely contain his excitement at being right and squirmed in his seat. "I told you! I told you!"

Frank started belly laughing. "All right, cornmeal it is. A barrel of cornmeal."

"I want an invitation to that fish fry." Madison smiled at them.

"Watch out or they'll put you to work," Lenny told her.

"For you guys, I'll charge double."

The fishermen had a good laugh at her, and Madison left to get a new pot of coffee.

This time, she had to brew it herself. She put in the tan paper filter, opened a packet of coffee grounds, dumped it in, shut the holder, and pressed the button to start it. While she waited, she cleared dishes off the counter. When she went to put them in the bus tubs, she saw that they were almost full. She lugged one off the shelf and went back to the dish room. The dish room had dirty dishes stacked high. She couldn't find Austin, the guy doing dishes. He had disappeared, so she started on the stack. She sprayed off the dishes and sent them through the machine as fast as she could. Austin came through the kitchen with containers from the walk-in cooler.

"Sorry, Madison. Benny is swamped and needed some things from the cooler."

"No problem, Austin. Help him with whatever he needs. I'll keep working on the stacks."

Madison checked her watch. She had another hour before meeting the realtor. She felt a lot calmer now, ready to face whatever she had to. Even the stacks of dishes in front of her. She grabbed another plate and rinsed it off.

CHAPTER 14

Jake flicked his hair out of his eyes. "You have to let it go, man."

"If I had known how rudely he would treat Madison, I never would have agreed to lunch at the café," Ryan said. He couldn't let it go.

"Dad was just being dad."

"That doesn't mean I have to like it."

"Life's too short to hold on to your anger."

Ryan knew his brother was right, but he wasn't about to admit it. Quiet filled the air a few minutes.

"I don't remember the resort. Have I been there before?" Jake asked.

Ryan ran through his memories. They didn't come often, but they had stayed in a cabin one summer. "I think so. I think Mom brought us out to spend a couple of weeks one summer. Dad didn't join us until the last weekend. I was probably twelve, so you would have been around five."

"Is that the time we had a frog in the house?"

Ryan laughed. "You remember the frog?"

"Sort of. I remember Dad in his boxer shorts yelling, holding it by its back legs. He took it to the front door and tossed it into the yard."

"I was in so much trouble, but I was crying for the poor frog. I thought if I kept it in a bucket in our room, no one would find it. It must have escaped and started hopping around."

"At least he let it go." Jake grinned.

"Yeah. He sure did. The frog flew better than a bird."

The brothers fell back into a comfortable silence. Soon they pulled onto the short gravel road running through the resort. Ryan parked by the house at the end of the lane. The front of the house held a one-room store offering items like bait and ice cream treats. A counter full of candy took up one side of the room and two restaurant style booths were in the back. Andy and Molly lived in the back of the house. It had three bedrooms and two bathrooms. His six cousins had shared two rooms between them all. The four boys had the largest bedroom set up with bunk beds. The girls fought too much over bunk beds and ended up with twin beds in the next bedroom. Andy and Molly shared the smallest bedroom.

The summer they had stayed there, Ryan couldn't believe you could fit so many people in such a small house. He didn't know what to think of his cousins running around in cut-off shorts and swimsuits. It didn't take long for them to pull Ryan into their world. Soon he was running around in his own shorts cut from a pair of jeans or his swimsuit, soaking up all the summer sun and summer fun he could manage. They'd start early in the morning trying to catch minnows near the shore and end late at night after a campfire with roasted marshmallows and s'mores.

The screen door to the store creaked when Ryan pulled it open and banged shut behind Jake.

"I'll be right with you," called a voice from the room behind the store. "Just a minute now." Andy entered the room and pushed his glasses back into place.

"Hi, Andy," Ryan greeted his uncle.

"Ryan! Jake! Come here and give me a hug. Molly! Molly, they're here!"

Molly came into the room with another round of hugs.

"Boys, it's been too long." Molly fussed over them. "Look at you! You've grown into men!"

"It happens to the best of us," Jake said as he leaned against the counter.

"It's great to see you, Molly," Ryan added. "It's been too long."

"Did you eat?" Andy asked.

"We have sloppy joes and cucumber salad if you're hungry," Molly said, motioning to the door that led to the house.

"We had lunch with Dad before we came," Ryan assured them.

"Is he here too?" Andy asked, his eyes widening.

"No, but he's looking forward to seeing you tomorrow." Ryan's face was smiling, but inside his stomach was in turmoil over the thought of telling his dad about the resort.

Molly snorted. "I'm sure he is."

"Now, Molly, it was nice of him to take time out of his busy schedule to come to our party."

Molly looked over the boys. "I'm glad he's spending time with you two."

"Well, Ryan, do you want to see what you're getting into?" Andy adjusted his baseball cap.

"I sure do." Ryan opened the door to the store.

"I have the side-by-side pulled up. Let's take a ride. Molly, my love, are you coming with us?"

"No, the girls are coming over in a few minutes. They want to go through the photo albums. I think they're hunting for pictures to share at the party tomorrow."

Ryan and Jake admired the utility vehicle before climbing in. They took off down the gravel road through the resort. They drove to the main road but instead of turning onto it, they drove straight across onto a trail worn into the long grass.

Andy pointed out towards the field. Raising his voice to be heard over the vehicle and wind, he started talking. "This is all rented out and paid up through the end of the year. The guy has been actively farming here, so the ground is okay with the nutrients. The PH is around six and he's been successful growing wheat. It's a bit difficult for him with the hill, but I hear that's good for grapes."

Ryan nodded, keeping a keen eye on the landscape.

"As you know, this side of the road is 40 acres. About 35 of them are farmland. There's a creek on the northeast side and some tree line. And here's the old house. There's no access to it, as you can see. You'll have to build up this path for a driveway of sorts. There's electric run out here, but the septic will need replacing."

He had seen pictures of the house, but Ryan marveled at what he saw. The old house looked bigger than Ryan had expected. Four tall white columns framed a bottom porch and an upper deck. The windows were large and intact, but the rest of the house would need a lot of work. The roof and wooden siding were worn beyond repair. He knew it had a dirt-floor basement. The entire house would have to be raised so they could lay a proper foundation.

Ryan could also picture his future winery. Not only the hill of grapes but also a wine bar for tastings and glorious gardens all around for people to picnic in.

Andy pulled up to the house and killed the engine. "Haven't been in here for about a year, but it's safe to walk through. Want a closer look?"

"Yes. Absolutely." Ryan nodded.

"This is a cool house. I can't believe it's hidden away back here," Jake said, climbing the stairs of the front porch.

"Yep." Andy started up again. "It was built in the 1890s. Other than that, no one knows much about it. The columns here are in pretty good shape, but the upper deck needs work."

Andy unlocked the padlock on the door and led them into the house. "Here's the front parlor. Off to the side, here is a study of sorts. The dining room is back here along with the kitchen. You saw the front stairwell coming in. You can probably save the oak banisters with a little care. Back here in the kitchen is the second stairwell. It's pretty tight, you'll either have to widen it or take it out."

The house didn't hold any furniture, but there were old cupboards in the kitchen and a heavy cast iron sink. With all of the windows, light flooded through the rooms. It was quiet, dusty, and cool.

"Now up here there's two bathrooms and four bedrooms. They're pretty good size, too. The main bedroom is in the front and has a little sitting room leading out onto the second deck."

"This looks like a house from a slasher movie," Jake said.

Ryan laughed. "Maybe now, but I can see it finished. It's going to be great."

He checked out all of the rooms, getting a good feel for the space. He had his phone out and took both pictures and notes as he went around opening and closing doors.

"These light fixtures are incredible. I hope we can use them."

"I bet if you find the right team, you can save a lot in this old house. Are you sure you want to go through with this? It's not my business, but renovating this house and planting a vineyard isn't the cheapest enterprise you could engage in. I've done all right with the resort but renting out this farmland helped pay the bills along the way."

"It's going to be an extensive project," Ryan said softly. "And I'm going to love every minute."

"I'll remember that when you're complaining about the price of everything from lumber to farming supplies," Jake said with a laugh.

"Anything else you want to see before we sign the papers?" Andy asked. "It's not too late if you want to back out."

"If you had them with you, I would sign them right now. Should we head back to the resort?"

"We sure can. After we wrap this up, I have some beers in the fridge. We can celebrate."

Ryan blinked at the sudden moisture threatening to spill from his eyes. He cleared his throat. "Sounds good, Andy."

When they returned to the resort, there were people everywhere. Molly sat in a camp chair surrounded by her children and their spouses. Grandchildren ran around the grounds the same as Ryan had when he was younger, wearing shorts and swimsuits and eating popsicles.

"Ryan? Is that you? And is that little Jake? Goodness, we haven't seen you in years!" Camille noticed them first. She didn't stop to let them answer. "Ryan, you're buying this old place? We couldn't be happier."

The crowd of relatives nodded and agreed.

"Are you ready to join us for a drink?" Molly asked. "We've been making Cloud Lake teas."

Ryan and Jake looked at each other.

"What's a Cloud Lake tea?" Jake asked, raising an eyebrow.

"It's like a Long Island, except Cloud Lake doesn't have an island. We add a splash of Blue Curaçao and call them Cloud Lake teas." Molly explained.

"I'm in." Jake replied, finding an empty chair to sit in.

"We better take care of business first. You boys will stay awhile though, right?" Andy asked.

Ryan looked at Jake and then nodded. He followed Andy into the store to get the paperwork signed. Ryan had already gone over a copy with a fine-tooth comb. He wanted to protect himself and his family. They were giving him a fair deal, and he didn't want anything to go wrong on either side.

"Here's a pen for you."

Ryan accepted the pen from Andy and signed his name. He had just finished his final real estate deal.

Grinning, he clapped his uncle on the shoulder. "Let's celebrate!"

Molly already had Cloud Lake teas made for them when they went back outside. Someone pulled more chairs out of the shed for them to sit down. Ryan settled in, took a long drink, and smiled. The drink tasted sweet, but it was cold and refreshing.

He thought about Madison and wished she was there, too. He wanted to tell her all about his day. As if she were magic, he saw her truck follow a sedan into the driveway. They pulled up next to the store before Andy noticed them.

"Uh oh," Andy said.

"What do you mean, uh oh?" asked Molly. "Is that Madison? And isn't that a realtor? Her face is on that billboard by the highway."

Ryan glanced from Molly back to Andy, wondering what was happening.

"I think her name is Sue something. She left a few messages, but I didn't think they were important. I hadn't called her back yet. I'll talk to them."

"Oh dear." Molly wrang her hands. "Madison said she wanted to buy the resort, but that was months ago. She's going to be so upset with us."

Ryan froze. "I thought she wanted to build an event center... for weddings and family reunions."

"Right." Molly nodded. "She wanted to build it right here. Back on the stretch of grass before the trees."

Jake muttered under his breath.

"What was that dear?" Molly asked.

Madison's truck and the sedan turned around and drove slowly out of the resort.

"I said game over. Ryan's been spending time with Madison."

"Oh, this is awful." Molly chewed at her bottom lip.

"Maybe I should go after her." Ryan rose from his chair.

"I'm staying here, bro. Give me your tea."

Ryan wanted to down the thing, but he handed it over to his brother. Holding his back rigid and straight, he walked to his car, refusing to hang his head. He'd find Madison and he would make her understand. This was just business. She didn't have to let it interfere with their burgeoning relationship. She would understand. She had to.

CHAPTER 15

Madison drove slowly out of the resort, taking care to avoid any of the children running around. She wanted to hit the gas and kick up gravel. She wanted to scream and cry and rant and rave, but she couldn't.

She pulled into the parking lot of the restaurant, turned her truck off and sat listening to the engine tick as it cooled off. She was numb. What was she going to do now? Chloe would be running the restaurant. She couldn't take the job back from her. Madison had been so careful and had done everything right. Ryan swooped in and bought the place with a cash sale. Cash. The money had been transferred. Andy said he was so sorry. It was over.

Laying her forehead against the steering wheel, she drew a deep, rattling breath. She listened to a car pull in and heard the car door slam. A knock sounded at her window. She inhaled deeply again and raised her head. Him.

Madison jumped out of her truck, slamming her door. "You. What are you doing here?"

"I'd like to talk to you."

Her voice rose as her frustration and disappointment spilled out of her. "I do not want to talk to you. There is nothing to talk about. Enjoy your resort." Madison stomped towards the back door.

"I did not know you were talking about the resort. This was just a business deal. Sometimes plans don't work out, but we can work around this."

Madison spun on her heel. Her voice lowered into a steely calm. "Right. Sometimes plans don't work out. I know I have to see you at the party tomorrow, but after that I never want to see you again."

"You're being unreasonable."

"Unreasonable? Unreasonable?" Madison yelled at full volume. "I have worked years for this. I worked sixty-plus hour weeks for this. I gave up friends and vacations and dreams for this."

Ryan lost his cool. "I too have worked years for this. I too have worked sixty-plus hour weeks for this. This my dream! And dammit, I deserve it!"

Benny came out of the employee entrance with his hands full of garbage bags. He watched them stare each other down. "Is everything all right?"

"Goodbye, Ryan." Madison said stiffly and walked through the door Benny had come out of.

She stomped through the kitchen, entered her office, and slammed the door shut. Leaning her back against the door, she slid until she sat on the floor. She sat there, staring blankly at the wall. It didn't take long for the knocking to begin.

"I'm not here."

The knocking continued.

"Go away." She said a little louder.

The knocking didn't stop.

She twisted around and cracked the door open. "What."

"I have strawberry milkshakes with sprinkles and french fries with gravy."

Madison scooted out of the way and Chloe pushed through the door.

She came in and sat on the floor next to Madison. She handed her a milkshake and set the fries between them.

"Aren't you supposed to be training Leah?" Madison stirred her whipped cream into her shake.

"That girl is running circles around me. She'll be fine for a few minutes. If she needs anything, she'll ask for help."

Madison and Chloe sat slurping their milkshakes and picking at the fries. Neither of them said anything for several minutes. Madison set her milkshake on the chair and burst into tears. Chloe moved the fries out of the way and put her arm around her friend. Chloe let Madison cry until her sobs slowed and she managed to take a long, rattling breath.

"He's not an out-of-towner. Not anymore."

"Who? Ryan? He said he was moving out here."

"Yes, Ryan. He swooped in here and bought the damn resort. I went out there. I had everything ready. Andy told me Ryan wanted the resort and he already sold it to him."

"Wow."

"Then he follows me out here and tells me it's just business."

"What did you say to him?"

"I said after tomorrow I never want to see him again."

"Harsh, but fair. Maybe I should do the catering tomorrow myself. I can ask Leah or someone if they're available to help. You can stay here and work with Benny."

"You've never run catering on your own."

"I can handle it."

"You're right. I know you can, but I should be there. I know it doesn't make much sense, but I have to face this. I have to face them. I feel like I've been hiding away and not facing things for too long. It's time to deal with reality."

"You're not going to spit in their food, are you?"

"Tempting, but no. I'm not really mad at Andy and Molly. I guess Ryan gave them a great deal. They get to stay on and run the resort, but Ryan is going to hire them some help. They're getting too old to do the heavy work that needs doing."

"But you're mad at Ryan?"

Madison fell silent while she thought about it.

"Maybe angry. Maybe disappointed. It's like there's one Ryan all about the business deal. Then there's this other Ryan underneath, all soft and sensitive. I let down my guard for the Ryan underneath, but today businessman Ryan showed up."

"At the risk of our friendship or having a milkshake poured over my head, may I make an observation?"

Madison's eyes narrowed at her friend. "I'm in a state. I make no guarantees."

Chloe nodded. "Fair. The thing is Madison, you and Ryan seem pretty similar. When your parents died and you took over the café, you were all business and work and staying cool, calm, and collected. In some ways, you still are. You work too many hours, and you try to take care everything by yourself. But I know underneath you are a wonderful friend. You are kind and caring and funny, but you don't make time for yourself or your friends or even your grandparents."

Madison was about to protest, but Chloe kept on.

"I know. You have lunch with them every week. They are here for an hour, and you sit with them for twenty minutes, tops. When was the last time you saw them outside of work?"

Madison's eyes filled with tears again. "I know. They deserve better."

"You deserve better too."

With that, Madison's tears spilled over. Chloe held her again and let her cry. Finally, the tears stopped flowing. Chloe pulled some napkins out of her apron.

"Clean yourself up, kid. You're a mess."

"I am." Madison blew her nose. "And I'm exhausted."

"You're going home. I can handle the restaurant."

Madison agreed. "First, I have to try to stand up. We've been sitting on the floor too long."

They helped each other up. Chloe gave Madison one last long hug and sent her on her way. Madison drove home but didn't stop at her driveway. She kept driving north until she arrived at her grandparents' place.

Her grandpa was mowing the lawn and her grandma was sweeping the deck. They stared at her in surprise. Grandma Mabel set down her broom and rushed over to give Madison a hug and say hello. Grandpa Don cut the motor and moved to stand behind Grandma Mabel.

"Beautiful girl!"

"Madison, what surprise. What are you doing here? Is everything okay? Come up on the patio and I'll get some iced tea."

Before Madison could say anything, Grandma Mabel disappeared into the house. Grandpa Don held out his elbow so she could loop her arm with his as they walked to the patio.

"Never can get a word in edgewise with her, but she makes some mighty fine iced tea."

Madison smiled and patted her grandpa's arm. "She's the best, and so are you."

They made themselves comfortable on the patio. Madison sat on the porch swing and her grandfather chose one of the porch chairs. They were wrought iron and had bright flowery cushions on them. The little matching tables set between them each had a pot of flowers in colors matching the cushions. For the longest time, Madison thought her grandma must have the best luck buying matching flowers every spring. It wasn't long ago that she learned her grandma sowed the seeds to grow the same types of flowers over and over again. The colors sometimes changed, but the flowers were always the same.

Grandma Mabel brought out the iced teas. She always made sure everyone had everything they wanted before she would settle into a seat herself. "Madison, it's so good to see you. Why, I don't remember the last time you popped in. Is everything all right?"

Madison steadied her breath and swallowed hard before telling them about losing the resort. She hesitated, unsure if she should tell them about Ryan, but those words spilled out of her, too. Her grandparents listened carefully as she poured her heart out to them.

Her grandpa reached over and patted her knee.

Grandma Mabel tried to comfort her. "I'm so sorry, dear. We know how much the resort meant to you. You've been working long and hard to buy that place. I have half a mind to call Molly and Andy and give them a piece of my mind."

Madison shook her head. "Don't you dare, Grandma. They didn't mean any harm. Ryan offered them more than I could have anyway."

"He is their blood relative, Mabel. That makes a difference too," Grandpa Don added.

"What is he going to do with the place? You said he was some sort of commercial real estate agent. What does he know about running a resort?" Grandma Mabel asked.

"I guess Andy and Molly are still going to run the resort. He told me about owning a winery. There's farmland attached to the resort. I planned to keep renting it out to the farmer who already rents it, but Ryan's going to take that over and grow grapes. He said something about a wine tasting room and gardens. I never put it together that he meant to buy the resort. I feel so stupid."

"You're not stupid, dear. He never mentioned buying the resort, or where he wanted this winery, did he?"

"Well, no."

"Oh, there's the phone. I'll be right back." Grandma Mabel disappeared into the house. It did not surprise Madison they still had a landline. They still struggled to use their cell phones.

Madison and Grandpa Don sat in silence together, occasionally sipping their drinks. Madison had the porch swing swaying back and forth. Soon she curled into the cushions and fell asleep. It was hours later that Grandma Mabel stood by her side, giving her a gentle shake.

"Madison. Madison, are you hungry? We're about to have supper. Grandpa grilled hamburgers and I made potato salad."

"How long have I been asleep?" She said rubbing at her eyes.

"Oh, a few hours now. It's nearly seven."

"Oh, gosh, the restaurant. I should go back in and help close."

"Nonsense. They would call if they needed you. You needed sleep and now you need to eat. We have watermelon too."

Madison couldn't argue with watermelon. Her stomach growled from her hunger. All she had today was her coffee and the milkshake and fries. She followed Grandma Mabel to the picnic table. Food and dishes filled every inch of it.

It had been too long since she'd joined her grandparents and had dinner together. They spent their time talking about trivial things like the weather and the restaurant. Grandpa Don teased her that the rain better hold off the next day so he could finish mowing.

After supper Madison helped bring everything in. She did the dishes with Grandma Mabel while Grandpa Don put away the food and cleaned the picnic table and grill. When they were all done, Grandma Mabel asked her to stay and watch their shows with them, but Madison needed to go home to sleep. She hugged them goodbye and left.

She was almost home when her phone rang. She looked at the caller ID and groaned. It was Molly. She debated if she should answer the phone or not while she pulled into her driveway and parked. Finally, she decided she couldn't avoid Molly forever, especially with the party tomorrow.

"Hello, Molly."

"Madison, hi. I finally have a moment alone and I had to call you. We feel terrible about what happened today. We really are very sorry."

"Thanks, Molly. I appreciate the call."

"Right. Again, we are terribly sorry and…"

Madison broke in. "We're still on for tomorrow, right? Everything is lined up and ready for your party."

"Yes, we're still on. I worried with what happened today…"

"There's nothing to worry about, Molly. It happened. It's just business." Madison winced as she said it. "That's all. We'll see you tomorrow, okay?"

"Thank you for being so understanding. And for tomorrow."

"You're welcome."

They said their goodbyes and hung up. Madison went into her little cabin and pulled her pajamas out of the closet. She went into the bathroom to take a shower, but she really wanted to soak in a bath. She would have to use a bathroom in the main house. Her shoulders dropped. She needed to let it go and stop caring so much. If she wanted a bath with bubbles and candles and soothing music, there was no reason she shouldn't use the main house. She gathered what she would need.

The house seemed too quiet and dark. She flipped on all the lights on the main floor and most of the lights on the second floor as well. The deep soaking tub in her parents' bathroom called to her. She ran the water until steam rose good and hot. She filled the tub as high as possible while she turned on some soft music. It had been years since she'd had a bubble bath. She sank into the sea of bubbles and soaked for over an hour before drying off and slipping into her pajamas.

She was warm and comfortable and didn't want to go out into the cool evening air. She stood considering her parents' bed. The sheets and coverlet had been recently washed, so they were fresh and clean. She slipped under the covers and fell asleep.

CHAPTER 16

Ryan turned off his alarm instead of waiting for it ring. He had hardly slept the previous night. The excitement of buying the resort, worrying about what Madison must think of him, and nervousness about telling his father the news had caused him to lie awake for hours. He had hoped to tell his father yesterday, but Scott and Danica didn't arrive home until late.

His shoulders were tight with tension. He decided to go for a run. Instead of running west towards the café, he ran north towards the resort. He kept his breathing even as his steps pounded the gravel on the side of the asphalt road. The crunching was rhythmic, but his mind was in chaos. He wanted to think through his next steps for moving to Cloud Lake. He avoided the thoughts about how his father would react when he finally told him the news. All he could think about was Madison. Her eyes had been fiery mad when she yelled at him. Her fists had balled up tight when she agreed that plans don't always work out. Her face had flushed red when she told him how hard she had worked. He felt awful about how things had happened.

When they had talked about their hopes and dreams, neither of them discussed concrete plans. They chatted more about the general ideas and how they could be successful. If only he had known she meant to buy the resort. But would he have done anything differently? He thought about their conversations as he ran.

He decided not. He still would have bought the resort, and he may even have intentionally kept it quiet so he could have an upper hand. Or he wouldn't have pursued Madison in the first place. Mixing business and pleasure often ended in disaster.

Still, he couldn't get over their night together. It had been so comfortable and easy. He craved that kind of cozy relationship. Instead of networking with business associates and clients, he wanted to have a genuine relationship with someone. No, not with someone, with Madison.

Ryan looped to the other side of the road and headed back to the cabin. He tried to think of ways he could patch up his relationship with Madison. Maybe they would never work out as a couple, but he hoped they could at least be friends. He wondered if she still planned to cater for his uncle and aunt's party. Maybe he could talk to her there. He had to make her see he hadn't meant to hurt her.

With another mile left to go, he thought about her plans for an event center. He could see the appeal. She talked about a barn-like structure, with a variety of lighting settings and a modern sound system. She had described a small but efficient kitchen and planned a small bar that would utilize the same storage space. She wanted a small comfortable room near the bathrooms for use as a dressing room for bridal parties. The whole place would have large windows, rustic woods, exposed beams, and, of course, expansive gardens.

Ryan had never been to the service club before, but his cousins had mentioned it. They described it as dark and joked about the wood paneling and worn yellowing fixtures. It didn't sound like the best place to hold a party, but his Aunt Molly had worried about summer rains ruining an outdoor get together.

In fact, the clouds were gray and heavy. The humidity clung to him as he ran. His shirt was soaking wet. He hadn't checked his weather app before he left, but the forecast had predicted afternoon showers. His aunt had the right idea when she'd planned for an inside party.

Ryan finished his run and headed in to take a shower. Opening the front door brought the smell of coffee and waffles. His dad and Jake were already at the breakfast bar, drinking coffee and eating the fruit that Danica always seemed to set out.

"I've just started the waffles. Shower quick if you want a hot one," Danica called out without turning around. She poured batter into a waffle maker.

Waffles sounded good to Ryan, and he hurried through a shower. It didn't take long for him to join the rest of them for breakfast.

"Pleasant run this morning?" Jake asked.

"Yeah, I needed a good run to think through everything."

"Boys! Have you been reading about these proposed tax hikes? The president is out of his mind! I tell you this economy is going to hell. They're talking some serious percentages here."

The boys watched Danica who had just sat down to eat.

"You know the idiom about death and taxes. I've read the worst of the tax increases have been tossed out. Either way, business is going well. I don't think your bottom line will take too big of a hit."

Scott grunted and went back to his waffles. Jake looked at Ryan and raised an eyebrow. Ryan got the message loud and clear.

"So, Dad." Ryan cleared his throat. "I have some news."

Scott put his tablet on the counter and peered at his son. "Oh? What's that?"

Ryan had rehearsed his speech so many times, but he couldn't seem to spit out the words.

Danica set her fork down and watched Ryan with curiosity. "Good news?"

"Well, you see, I quit my job. Next week is the last week I'm obligated to work out of the office. I may still have a few loose ends to wrap up, but I can take care of the rest remotely."

"That's great news, son. Now you can come work for me. I wish you would have said something sooner. We'll have to get an office arranged for you."

"No. Dad. Thanks for the offer, but I'm heading in a different direction." Ryan looked his dad in the eye. "I bought Andy and Molly's resort and I'm going to use the farmland to start a winery."

Scott's mouth dropped open.

"Congratulations!" Danica said and patted his hand. "A winery sounds fantastic. How many acres did you buy?"

"That side of things is about forty acres."

"What a great start for a boutique winery. I hear they have quite a few grape varieties that work well around here. Have you started sourcing your vines?"

"Now wait a minute. Wait just a damn minute here. You bought that fleabag resort? For how much? What the hell is going on with you? Is it that damn girl you've started mooning over?" Scott's face grew red with his rising anger.

"This has nothing to do with Madison."

"Then you tell me why you're throwing your career away, your life away, to move out to the middle of nowhere!"

"Scott." Danica's voice was quiet but stern. Ryan didn't think his dad even heard her.

"Don't you 'Scott' me! This is between me and Ryan. This is the most asinine damn thing you could come up with. You did this just to throw it in my face, didn't you? What is wrong with you, boy?"

"Nothing is wrong. I want..."

"Want? What could you possibly want? Your mother and I provided everything you needed to get on the right track. Your career is successful. You have a nice house in the right neighborhood. The only thing you should want is a wife and some kids. Not a run-down resort and a damn field of dirt."

A switch flipped inside of Ryan. Instead of being afraid of his dad's temper, he pitied him. Instead of standing there feeling like a disappointment, he spoke up.

"You need to stop yelling. I will not discuss this with you until you calm down. I will say, this is my life, my dream, and I don't have to defend myself to anyone."

Anger still flushed red in his father's face. "Get out."

"Scott." Danica's voice was sharper this time.

"Do not 'Scott' me again or you're out on your ass too. You heard me boy. Get out!"

"Fine. I'll pack and leave."

Jake had been sitting between Scott and Ryan for the entire exchange. His head had whipped back and forth as if he had been watching a tennis match. He cleared his throat and stood up.

"I'm out, too."

Scott's expression betrayed his outrage, but he didn't say another word. He went out, slamming the back door and made his way down to the lake.

No one spoke for a moment.

"Danica, I'm sorry we dragged you into our argument." Ryan lowered his eyes to the floor.

"I'm not worried. Besides, I get a bonus every time he threatens to fire me. If he actually does fire me, I get a substantial severance package. Let him cool off a little. I'll talk to him."

"Thanks. For everything."

The brothers went to their respective wings and packed as fast as possible. When they came out minutes later, Danica stood out on the back patio watching Scott. Scott still looked angry and red-faced while he paced and ranted at the lake. Ryan led the way out the door.

"Where are you going?" Jake asked.

"I'll stay with someone at the resort. I hope there's a free bed and I don't end up on a couch. How about you? Are you heading out there too?"

"No, I texted Jesse. I can stay at his place tonight. We were going tubing tomorrow, anyway."

"See you at the party?"

"I'll be there."

Ryan felt a little jealous of his brother. He wished he could have texted Madison. He would even sleep on her lounger again. Instead, he drove to the resort to find someplace to sleep after the party.

The resort looked peaceful when he pulled in. He went into the store and yelled hello. Molly came out of the back, wiping her hands on a towel.

"What are you doing here so early? Is everything all right?"

"I finally told Dad about the resort."

"Oh dear. I take it things didn't go well."

"No. Not at all. Do you have an extra bed around here?"

"You know, the kids all took the cabins so they would have room for their own kids. Their rooms here are open. You can take a bunk in the boys or if you can stand all the pink, you're welcome to the girls."

"I'll take a bunk. That sounds great. Thanks Molly."

She came over and hugged him tight. "You're always welcome here. Whether or not you own the place."

Ryan chuckled. "It doesn't seem real yet."

"Well, it takes time. You'll have enough reality next spring when you're digging in the dirt planting grape vines."

"I can't wait." Ryan grinned. "Where is everyone?"

"The menfolk went golfing and the ladies went to decorate the service club."

"And the kids?"

"They divided and conquered," Molly said. "They took all of them with, half golfing, half decorating. I'm about to join the ladies. They told me they would take care of everything, but it's too quiet around here! You're welcome to join me."

"I don't think Camille and Patricia consider me one of the girls," Ryan said with a laugh.

"You could catch up with the golf crew. They might even be playing instead of drinking this early."

"I think I'll stay here and go for a swim."

"All right then. We'll be back around lunchtime. They're grilling today. They have brats, hot dogs, and corn. I saw a few watermelons around too."

"Sounds wonderful."

"Can you do me a favor? I really hate to ask, but I'm running behind today. Madison had ordered a flat of buns for us. She gets a better rate than the grocery store. Would you pick them up for me?"

Ryan must have made a face.

"It's fine. I talked to her and apologized. Everything is all right now. She said it was just business. Isn't that nice?"

He struggled with his thoughts. Would Madison be mad? Would she talk to him? He gave in to his aunt. "Sure, I can pick them up."

Ryan hauled his suitcase and briefcase into the boy's bunkroom. The room hadn't changed much since they were kids. There were homemade jean quilts on the beds. A single nightstand with a lamp shaped like a boat – complete with fisherman – stood between the bunk beds. The walls had wooden figures of fish that the boys had glued googly eyes on. Plastic stars scattered across the ceiling.

He thought of his own room as a child. He'd had a queen-sized bed and a duvet with a blue cover. Framed and matted pictures of purebred dogs hung over his bed, even though they had never had a dog. The large desk always held the latest computer. In the corner stood a fern he never thought about. The housekeeper must have watered it, or maybe it was silk.

Ryan ran his fingers through his hair. Scott said they provided Ryan with everything. They did provide for him. He had nice clothes. They bought his first car. He went to excellent schools. Sill, looking around the bunk room, he knew he missed out on a lot of love that his parents hadn't been able to provide.

CHAPTER 17

Madison tried to concentrate on the order. Two eggs over medium, white toast, a side of bacon, and coffee. It wasn't a difficult order, but she had to ask twice before she gave in and wrote it down. She was trying hard to get through the day and then the weekend. She would deal with everything Monday when she had the day off. There would be time to think things through and decide what she wanted to do next. For now, she needed to finish entering this order and move on to the next customer.

The wait to be seated at the café kept getting longer and they were short staffed. The morning server, Rachel, caught strep throat from her brother who caught it at day camp, so she called in sick. Tate, one of the dishwashers, had broken his arm skateboarding and would be out for weeks. Chloe was 20 minutes late, and Madison had no idea where she was. She wanted to call Landon in to help with the dishes, but without two servers, she couldn't get to a phone.

She was about to take another order when she noticed a commotion at the host stand. The hostess, Dusty, stood arguing with

Gladys, who had a very wiggly purse. Madison excused herself from the table and went to the host stand.

Gladys didn't see her approach and wheedled Dusty to let Jameson in. "He really is very small. We had a nice long walk and I'm sure he'll sleep through brunch. Look! My friends are waiting for me to sit with them." She waved to her friends, who waved back at her. "He won't be any trouble. He'll stay in my purse here." She saw Dusty looking past her shoulder and turned to see what she was looking at.

Madison greeted her with a smile. "No. Absolutely not. Gladys, you know Jameson can't come in."

"He gets so lonely in the car."

"I'm sorry, but the answer is no. It's always a no. Please do not try to bring him in here again. You know the rules."

"All right. I'll put him out there. It will just take me a minute. I'll be right back in."

Madison smiled at Dusty. "Thanks for stopping her. I know it isn't always easy."

"She just doesn't stop talking. She has so many excuses for why that dog should come in. It's as if she thinks if she talks long enough, people will get tired of listening to her and give in."

"She sure does. But you did a good job."

"Thanks, but I'm glad you came over when you did."

"That's what I'm here for."

Dusty had a moment with no new customers coming and dashed off to collect used menus. Madison went back to the kitchen to bring an order out. Chloe breezed in, tying her apron as she walked through the kitchen.

"Chloe! What happened? You didn't call."

"Sorry, boss. I got a flat. Took me forever to get the lug nuts off. I thought I texted." Chloe checked her phone. "Oh no. I'm sorry. I didn't hit send."

"I'm glad you're here now. We're swamped. It's only been me and Leah. Take the lakeside section so Leah can stay between us. She's doing great, but she might need something or have questions for us."

"Where's Rachel?"

"Sick with strep."

Chloe's eyes wandered over the dish station. "No one's on dishes?"

"Broke his arm skateboarding."

"You could try calling Landon," Benny said, pointing a spatula at Madison.

"It's on my to-do list. I have to get this order out or they'll complain about cold eggs."

Madison took the order up front to deliver it. Chloe let Dusty know she could start seating her section. Dusty went up front to take the names of the customers coming in and seat the next group. Instead of seating Chloe, she sat them in Madison's section. Madison would have to remind Dusty not to skip in the seating rotation. Chloe should have been sat first.

She went to greet the table and saw why they were sitting in her section. It was her ex again.

"Hello, Jonah. And it's Kassidy, right?"

The girl nodded but continued staring at the menu. Madison thought she was extraordinarily pretty but couldn't figure out why she wouldn't say anything. It seemed strange.

"It's so good to see you again. I'm glad you're our waitress this time. We hardly had a chance to reconnect last time we were in."

"Right. Well, it is pretty busy today so I don't have a lot of time to catch up, but what can I get you to drink? Coffee? Juice?"

"There's always time for old friends, isn't there?"

Madison tried to smile. "Of course. Can I get you started with some coffee?"

"I'll have coffee and orange juice. Kassidy will have green tea if you have it."

At least Kassidy looked her in the eye when she nodded.

"We do. Do you want honey?"

Again, Kassidy nodded.

"Great. I'll be right back with your drinks."

Madison thought Chloe would come over and chat in the wait station, but Chloe was busy with a table in her section. Leah hustled a food order out to one of her tables. Madison wouldn't have talked to Leah about her ex, anyway. She didn't know her that well. Madison would have to take care of Jonah and his girlfriend and talk to Chloe about it later. She readied their drinks and returned to their table.

"Here we are. I brought cream for the coffee and honey for the tea. Were you two ready to order or did you need a few minutes?"

"We're all ready. Hey, remember the time I tried to make you breakfast? We started making out, and I forgot all about the eggs. They burned so bad they set the fire alarms off!"

Madison stood and stared at him. Mortified, she answered slowly, "Yes. I remember. I had to throw out the pan."

"What a morning."

Kassidy's left eye twitched like she wanted to roll her eyes but was holding herself back.

Madison cleared her throat. "So, I can recommend the pancakes or an omelet."

"Oh yes, I'll have an all-meat omelet with pancakes and Kassidy wants two eggs over easy and wheat toast."

"Sounds good. I'll get your order right in for you."

Madison walked away as fast as she could without running. She entered the order and went back to the kitchen to run other orders out to the customers seated at the counter. She took the coffeepot around to fill mugs. A few customers needed little things, a side of ketchup, more creamers, extra napkins, a new fork because they had dropped one. She had no time to stop. She needed to get back and run some dishes, but there wasn't time to spare.

Leah was doing great. She was efficient and friendly. The customers took to her right away and she did an excellent job waiting on them. She seemed to be born to waitress.

Chloe was having a blast waiting on her tables. She flitted around but kept flitting over to a table full of guys. She must have been joking with them because she had them laughing loudly with her when she stopped at their table.

Benny came out to fill his coffee mug while Madison started the other coffee maker. He looked sweaty and tired.

"Are you doing okay, Benny?"

"I needed a minute. Austin's helping me cook, but he's also trying to get some dishes done before we run out. It's crazy today."

"I agree. I wish I could get back to help you, but we're short up here too."

A laugh erupted from the table Chloe waited on.

Benny glanced over and frowned.

"It's okay. I have the kitchen covered. I know my place." His voice sounded sour.

Madison didn't have time to ask Benny what he meant. She had to clean off a table so the next couple waiting could have a seat and she had to deliver Jonah and Kassidy's orders.

"Here's your all-meat omelet and here are your eggs, over easy, and wheat toast. Is there anything else you need right away?"

"The food looks great. You're looking good too, Madison."

Then everything exploded at once. Austin came up to her, soaking wet from head to toe, and told her the dishwasher exploded.

Kassidy muttered, "I'm so over this." She took her plate of eggs and dumped it over Jonah's head, threw his orange juice in his face, and stomped out of the restaurant. She peeled out of the parking lot in the car they had come in.

Jameson started barking, fought his way out of the purse Gladys had him in and ran around the restaurant at full speed.

And Ryan walked in.

Madison went into overdrive. "Austin, underneath the dishwasher is a water shut-off valve. Make sure it gets shut off. I'll call a handyman in a minute. Gladys, get a hold of that dog. If I see him in here again, I will ban you. Permanently. Jonah, get yourself cleaned up in the bathroom. This is Ryan. He's leaving and can give you a ride somewhere."

Austin ran back to the kitchen to turn off the valve. Gladys grabbed her dog, threw enough cash to pay for her meal on the table, and left in a huff. Jonah went to the bathroom. Ryan stood there, shocked.

He regained his composure. "Molly sent me. She said you had a flat of hotdog buns for her."

"Pull around to the back. You can load up back there. I'll be there in a minute." Madison inhaled sharply. "Okay, everyone. Shows over. Give us a moment to reset and we'll be right with you. Coffee is on us this morning."

Madison headed towards the back door and pulled out her phone. She thumbed through until she found Dylan's number. She propped open the back door.

"Hello, Dylan?"

She grabbed the bread rack and pulled off a flat of hotdog buns. Holding the phone between her ear and her shoulder so she could hear Dylan's "Hello, Madison. What's up?"

"Sorry to call you on a Saturday."

Dylan told her it was no problem and asked what he could do for her as she brought the flat out to Ryan's SUV.

"Our dishwasher went crazy. Can you come take a look?"

Ryan climbed out of the car and opened the back hatch while Dylan asked her what was wrong with it.

"I'm not sure. I think Austin got the water shut off, but I didn't get a chance to ask him what happened."

Dylan explained he had to find someone to watch little D.J. so he could come out while Ryan took the bags of buns and loaded them into an empty tote he had in his car.

"Uh-huh." Madison replied.

Then he explained that he would have to charge weekend rates even though they were friends while Ryan closed up his hatch and stood staring at Madison.

"Uh-huh. Great. I'll you soon then. Thanks Dylan."

"So. I'm giving some guy a ride?"

Jonah came through the door a little cleaner and a little stormy.

"Yes, this is Jonah. He's my ex-boyfriend. You probably saw his girlfriend tear out of the parking lot as you came in. Jonah, this is Ryan, my never-going-to-be-my boyfriend. He'll give you a ride to your mom's or wherever. I don't care if you both end up in Antarctica. I have to get back in there. Goodbye." She resisted the urge to add a "good riddance" at the end.

Neither of them made a sound as Madison walked back into the restaurant and slammed the kitchen door. She tried to feel bad about putting them together and sending them away, but she didn't. She couldn't believe how badly Jonah had behaved. If she could have gotten away with it, she would have cheered for Kassidy when she gave it to him and stalked off. The girl had more moxie than she let on. She also couldn't believe Ryan would show his face at the café. She thought she had been crystal clear about not wanting to see him.

Find someone to fancy. Madison wanted to spit as the thought crossed her mind. If she hadn't been in the café, she might have. A relationship may have worked for her grandma and grandpa – they had a long happy marriage. However, if these were the men she had to choose from, she was going to stay alone and be happy about it.

CHAPTER 18

Jonah and Ryan eyed each other warily, especially with the way that Madison had introduced them. Ryan gave in first. He cleared his throat and offered his hand to Jonah.

"Nice to meet you. You need a lift?"

Jonah still eyed Ryan coolly but shook his hand. "I guess I'm heading to my mom's."

They sat in complete silence, trying to ignore each other as much as possible. Jonah did have to give Ryan directions as they drove past the lake towards town.

"You're not on the lake?" Ryan asked.

"No. My mom has a double-wide outside of town. Right before you get to the grocery store."

"Sure." Ryan had no clue where the grocery store was. He hadn't gone into town yet.

The silence hung in the air between them for a few more minutes until Jonah looked over at Ryan.

"What did you do to Madison?"

Ryan frowned. "I didn't do anything to her."

"You ticked her off." Jonah chuckled.

"I did, yes. I bought the Cloud Lake Resort. I didn't know she wanted to buy it."

Jonah's eyes grew wide. He threw his head back and laughed. "And I thought I was an asshole to her."

"Why? What did you do to her?"

"I left her the day before her parents' funeral. It wasn't my finest moment."

Ryan didn't know how to respond. He wanted to yell at the guy. Ryan wasn't a violent person, but he wanted to punch him. From the looks of the guy, it didn't seem to be the best choice he could make.

Jonah must have noticed Ryan's hands tighten on the steering wheel.

"I told you I'm an asshole. I had a girl on the side too. If you're going to punch me, can you wait until we're out of the car?"

"I'm not going to punch you."

Jonah gave him a nod. "Good to know."

The rest of the drive fell back into an intense silence. They arrived at the mobile home park. Jonah didn't open the door right away.

"Thanks for the ride."

"You're welcome," Ryan said through gritted teeth as he looked over at Jonah. He wanted the guy out of his SUV. Jonah still had his hand on the door handle.

"Look, Madison is a tough one, but she's a good girl. Treat her better than I did."

After Jonah got out and slammed the door shut, Ryan answered him. "I intend to."

When Ryan returned to the resort, he put the buns in the kitchen and headed for the bunk room. He needed to get physical to release all the tension building up inside of him. His emotions were too messy to deal with. It was too hot to run, but the cool water of the lake called to him. He dug a swimsuit out of his suitcase and changed out of his clothes.

The water seemed cold at first compared to the hot and humid summer air, but he soon acclimated to it. He wanted to swim across the lake, but decided it wasn't a wise choice when no one else was around. He swam along the shoreline. Instead of swimming hard and fast like he planned, he swam slower along the reeds.

He came across a patch of water lilies and stopped to tread water. He'd never seen real water lilies before. He swam along and found a log full of turtles sunning themselves, but he splashed too loud, and they all slid off the log into the water. Slowly and methodically, he swam back to the resort.

Ryan floated on his back and watched the white puffy clouds. He tried to think of what he could say to Madison. She was unreasonable and stubborn, but he wanted a second chance. He wasn't ready to give up on her yet. He didn't know how he could make her see his side of the matter. She had to realize he needed this. Besides, she still had the restaurant. He hadn't taken away her livelihood or anything all that catastrophic.

Cars began pulling into the resort. Ryan waded up to the shore and back onto dry land. He grabbed a beach towel, dried off, and pulled on a polo shirt. A thought that he should really buy some T-shirts crossed his mind. His cousins and their families came pouring out of the cars. Patricia walked over to him and handed him her sleeping toddler.

"Here, take Liam. If I set him down, he's going to wake up. I'm going to get the Cloud drinks going while the guys start the grills."

Activity blossomed everywhere. Some people were setting up chairs. There were a few getting the grills lit. Others brought out platters of food. Children ran around everywhere.

Patricia's husband Blake found Ryan holding the sleeping Liam and laughed at him.

"He's a baby, not a bomb. You're not going to hurt him."

"I don't think I've ever held a kid before," Ryan admitted.

"You're doing fine, but I can take him if you want."

"No, we're all right. Just let him sleep."

They found a couple of empty chairs.

"No grill duty for you?" Ryan asked.

"One Thanksgiving, I tried to deep fry the turkey and it caught on fire. I'm not allowed around the food anymore."

Ryan laughed.

"So, you really bought this place?" Blake asked.

"I did. I'll be moving out here in a week."

"Are you going to live here at the resort?"

"I'll stay in the green cabin to start. It has a heater to get me through the winter. The farmland has an old house past the tree line across the road. My plan is to restore that and live there once it's done."

"That's incredible. I don't think I ever knew there was farmland attached to this place."

"I'm surprised none of you wanted to buy it."

"I think we all thought about it, but the resort is such a huge commitment. We enjoy our eight-to-five-and-home-in-time-for-supper work lives. Patricia and her siblings are glad it won't be torn down and made into condos though."

"I won't let that happen. I'm still not sure what I'll do when Andy and Molly fully retire, but I don't plan to change this place much. My focus is across the road."

His cousin Aaron came and sat with them. "Are you talking about your plans? Are you going to restore the old house?"

Ryan answered the same questions over and over as more people came to sit and ask him about his plans. Patricia came back for Liam and handed Ryan a Cloud Lake tea. Those that were grilling finished cooking, and everyone piled their plates full of food. Everyone seemed happy and chatted, teased, and laughed with each other. Ryan loved every minute of it.

He felt comfortable, as if he belonged. His nerves weren't frayed from waiting for his father to explode. He wasn't anxious about the people he was sitting with judging him and his business acumen. They were interested in what he was saying, and he enjoyed what they had to say.

Still, his mind kept wandering back to Madison. Her plans were so different for the resort, and she knew his cousins and their families much better than he did. She'd gone to school with the youngest three. He wondered if she ever had a Cloud Lake tea and if she enjoyed them.

He visited with the family late into the afternoon until Molly started encouraging everyone to get ready. She didn't want to be late to her own party. When she was satisfied her family would get ready on time, she went in to get ready as well.

Ryan appreciated having a bathroom to himself, even if it had a tiny shower. He needed to wash off the smell of the lake and get into nicer clothes. Before heading into the shower, he pulled out a white button-down shirt and a pair of chinos. He'd never worn them, but the salesgirl had insisted he wouldn't regret buying them.

The weather had cooled, and the clouds had darkened while Ryan got ready. His cousin Aaron offered him a seat in their car and Ryan gladly accepted. He didn't want to find his way in a storm. They were the only ones with room in their car. They had their 4-year-old, Bennet, in a car seat in the back next to Ryan. Aaron's wife, Ellie, was five months pregnant with their second baby. She offered to drive since Aaron and Ryan had drunk a few Cloud Lake teas during the afternoon.

They made it to the parking lot of the service club before lightning cracked through the sky. They ran to the doors and opened them as the fat raindrops started pelting the ground.

"Wow, look at the rain." Bennet said. His eyes were wide, and he clutched Ellie's hand.

"Come here sport." Aaron picked him up. "Let's go find some seats."

They were in a sort of entryway with dark wooden benches along the sides and fake plastic trees by the windows. The doors to the hall were open, and Ryan could see dark paneling and party lights. The stage at the far end was set up for a band. Giant golden balloons shaped into the number 50 floated on one side of the stage and a large bouquet with a golden ribbon reading "Forever in Love" stood on the other side.

A table had been set aside for Andy and Molly with a garland of flowers and electric candles that flickered with a soft light. The rest of the tables were round and held flower centerpieces. A cake table and a present table were tucked off to one side. Even though the invites said, "Your presence is present enough," people had brought gifts. Ryan noted a few wine-bottle sized gift bags and grinned.

Ryan walked by the buffet line hoping to read Madison's mood. The food smelled amazing, and he scanned the tables. The first table held caprese salad skewers, candied bacon, and goat cheese crostini along with a regular fruit bowl and veggie tray. The main table was filled with a salad of greens, candied carrots, and roasted potatoes. For the main entrée, there was a choice of chicken cordon bleu, five-cheese penne pasta, or prime rib.

Madison stood at the end, carving the prime rib. She avoided his eyes. Beyond the buffet Chloe manned a small bar and glowered at Ryan every time their eyes met. Ryan was debating getting in line for dinner and a drink or just sitting down when he caught sight of Jake and Jesse. They were soaked through from the rain. He went over to say hi.

"You two look like drowned rats."

"Hey bro. It's coming down bad out there."

"The lightning is crazy too," Jesse said while he surveyed the puddles his shoes were making.

"Have you eaten yet?" Jake asked.

"No." Ryan's eyes slid over to Madison and his heart ached. Was it really over before it even had a chance to begin?

"Let's go," Jesse said. "I love it when Madison caters. Did she do the candied bacon tonight?"

"Yeah, and then some," Ryan replied. His palms were starting to sweat, and his jaw hurt from clenching his teeth. He was anxious about interacting with Madison.

They headed over to the line for the buffet table. Ryan figured there was safety in numbers. When they moved to the end of the line, Madison no longer stood there. A server Ryan didn't know had taken her place. With their plates full, they found seats with Aaron and Ellie. Little Bennet had his plate piled high with fruit and pasta, which he insisted was mac and cheese.

"Little dude isn't wrong," Jake said. "Hey, we forgot drinks." Jake and Jesse looked at Ryan.

Ryan sighed. "I'll get them, but you better not touch any of my bacon while I'm gone."

He stood in line at the bar. He actually wished the line would move slower, but Chloe was quick and efficient. Ryan soon stepped up to her counter.

"You."

"Yes."

"I was wrong about you. It doesn't happen often, but I guess anything is possible." She looked at him like he was gum on the bottom of her shoe.

Ryan kept his face passive. "I see."

"What are you drinking?"

"Two craft beers and bourbon neat."

"Can I see your ID?"

"Are you serious? We've been at the bar together twice."

"Anyone who looks under thirty-five needs to be carded."

Ryan took out his wallet and showed her his driver's license.

"Fine. That will be $100 please." Chloe smiled at him primly.

"For two beers and a bourbon? What, is the bourbon twenty years old and single barrel aged?"

"No, the drinks are $20. The rest is an idiot tax."

Ryan threw a $50 on the bar. "I'm not the only idiot around here."

He took the drinks and stalked back to the table. They had left his bacon alone, but he had lost his appetite. He took a drink of his bourbon instead. These women were impossible.

"Oh, look. Your dad's here." Aaron gestured his fork towards the door.

Scott appeared to be reluctant to enter the room. Ryan couldn't tell if he had brought Danica with him or if she had prodded him to get there. With determination, she steered him towards their table. He stood in front of the table and shifted on his feet, not making eye contact with anyone. Danica gave him a small nudge with her elbow.

"Mind if we join you?"

Jake and Ryan eyed each other, and Ryan shrugged.

"Sure, grab another chair. We can make room for two." Jake smiled.

Everyone scooted a little closer together.

Ellie must have noticed the tension. "If you'll excuse us. I think we're ready for cake. Want to get a piece of cake Bennet?"

"Yes! Cake! What kind?"

"I don't know. Let's go find out."

"Cake sounds good." Jesse followed them over to the cake table.

Scott watched them walk away. "Boys, I think I owe you an apology. I..." His voice trailed off as he gathered his thoughts. "Ryan, I'm sorry. What I said earlier. I worry about you boys. I shouldn't have lost my temper with you."

Ryan gazed at his dad. Scott looked older. Ryan saw more wrinkles around his eyes and gray blending in with his dad's blonde hair. Instead of being the picture of wealth and power, he seemed worn and tired.

"Thanks, dad. Apology accepted." His dad had never apologized before, and Ryan knew it must have taken a lot for him to admit he was wrong.

CHAPTER 19

Madison stood at the end of the buffet. There were a few people still coming through the line, but almost everyone had eaten. She always worried there wouldn't be enough food, but there had been plenty. Soon she would pack the leftovers for Andy and Molly to bring home. Because Rachel was still sick, Dusty had agreed to help out. She watched her walk around clearing off tables.

Catering the party had been another success, but Madison wasn't feeling it. The day had been long and miserable, and she wanted to go home. She planned to take a long shower, put on her softest pajamas and crawl under the quilt for a long, hard sleep. She wanted to ask Chloe to open the restaurant in the morning, but they would be working late. Madison didn't think it would be fair to even ask her.

She tried not to, but her eyes kept wandering over to Ryan. He looked different. He wore his hair naturally instead of brushing it back. His tan had deepened from his time in the sun. He seemed more relaxed. When they first met he was like a tightly wound spring, and now he seemed at ease. Everything seemed to be going his way while Madison's plans had all gone wrong.

She shook her head. She would figure something out. There had to be something else for her to work on. There was more to life than the restaurant.

Madison checked on Chloe. "How's the bar business?"

"I'm killing it. I have to keep emptying the tip jar. It's been overflowing. Even splitting it three ways we'll have plenty of bar money."

"I don't think I'll be in a bar mood for a while. I'll put mine away for a rainy day."

Chloe nodded solemnly. "Except it's raining today." Her face brightened. "It's time for the speeches! This is my favorite part."

Someone had brought Andy a microphone, and he fumbled to turn in on. He tapped it a few times to make sure it worked. He cleared his throat.

"I want to begin by thanking each and every one of you for joining us today. Molly and I are thrilled you would celebrate this momentous occasion with us. This party is incredible.

"Molly, you're incredible. I've been married to this beautiful woman for fifty amazing years, and she is still my best friend. Like anyone, we've had our ups and downs, but we were able to rely on each other. We are always there for each other. We helped each other through.

"We had to. Raising our six children and running the resort made life interesting at times. Some days we were so busy we didn't know if we were coming home to cook dinner or going out to watch one of the kids playing baseball. Our lives have been full and blessed."

Tears started to prickle Madison's eyes.

Andy continued. "When we first started out together, we were young. Molly was eighteen years old, and I was only nineteen.

We went to college together. I studied law and Molly studied to be a nurse. We'd come out to Cloud Lake in the summers to spend time with Molly's family. We stayed at the Cloud Lake Resort with them. Then one day it went up for sale. We snatched it up as soon as we could and moved out here. I think I still have a box of old law books collecting dust in the attic, and I don't regret it one bit. Well, maybe I regret they're still up there. I should have thrown them out ages ago."

The crowd laughed.

"The thing of it is, the lake, this community, the life Molly and I built together, it's better than anything I could have dreamed of. Every boat ride, every sunset, every smile has been worth more to me than any career in law could have provided.

"Molly, I love you more than life itself. You mean everything to me. Camille, Aaron, Patricia, Manny, Kevin, and Herman, thank you and your families so much for throwing us this wonderful party. You kids are fantastic, and we love you with all of our hearts. And to the rest of our friends and family, thanks again for joining us to celebrate.

"Anyway, I don't have too much more to say, but we do have an announcement to make. We've sold our beloved resort to our nephew, Ryan. Molly and I aren't so young anymore. We're planning to retire in a few years. In the meantime, Ryan has some grand plans he's working on while he's helping us out. We're happy to announce that the Cloud Lake Resort will remain a resort for many years to come."

Applause erupted around the room. Madison bit her lip. She refused to cry in front of all these people. Chloe grabbed her hand and squeezed it, but she didn't dare look her friend in the eye."

Andy handed Molly the microphone and kissed her cheek.

"Wow! Fifty years! When did we get so old? I still remember the day Andy and I met. I was working at the movie theater. Back then, we had the cutest little uniforms, and I thought I looked so glamorous. Andy and his friends came up to me to buy popcorn and sodas. When his friends went in to watch the movie, he stayed behind to flirt with me. I think he missed half the show before I could shoo him away. He came back every Saturday, and every Saturday he missed the first half of the movie hanging out around my counter. I told him he should try watching a whole movie sometime. What fun could it be to watch half a movie? He said he'd watch a whole movie if I agreed to join him. We went to the movies the next Friday, and the rest is history.

"We've had a wonderful lifetime together. Not because everything was perfect, not every day is full of sunshine, but because we had each other. We've been committed since the beginning. Our love grew because we learned to be kind and to forgive one another."

Madison whispered to Chloe. "I don't know if I can handle this."

"Through teamwork and respect, we built a beautiful life for us and our children and their children. Andy, thank you for being my partner, my friend, my husband, and my rock. I love you and our life together."

Andy wrapped Molly in a hug. They were both misty-eyed and dabbing at the corners of their eyes. Applause, whistles, and congratulations came from all over the room.

Madison's heart ached. She missed her parents so much. She still couldn't believe they were gone. They didn't get to celebrate any more anniversaries. They didn't get to appreciate their future grandchildren.

"I need a few minutes," she told Chloe. The tears were threatening to spill hot and heavy.

Chloe bobbed her head in agreement. With the band warming up, people were lining up at the bar again. Madison slipped away through the crowd. There wasn't any place with privacy, so she risked the rain and went outside.

The driving rain was coming down hard and fast, whipping around from swift gusts of winds. Lightning crackled through the sky with great booming thunder. The storm outside was nothing to what was going on inside Madison's heart. Her emotions ran wild.

She was still so angry about losing her parents that she wanted to scream at the sky. She didn't want to run the restaurant anymore, but she also couldn't let it go. If felt like letting her parents go. This new project had meant so much to her. It was a way of moving on and doing something she wanted to do. It was something she had been excited about and now the chance was gone. She didn't want to live the life her parents' deaths had trapped her in anymore.

Hot, angry tears spilled down her cheeks. Her throat burned from the raw emotions churning inside. Blindly, she made her way to her truck to get out of the rain. Her keys were still inside. She sank to her knees in the gravelly muck of the parking lot and sobbed.

Her tears finally subsided, leaving her exhausted. She didn't want to go back in. All she wanted was to go home and get warm again. Soaking wet, cold, and muddy, she pulled her phone out of her back pocket to message Chloe. Maybe Dusty would bring her purse out so she wouldn't have to go back inside.

Her phone was full of missed messages. She had left her phone on silent while she worked. She scrolled back through them.

Everything is gone

This is awful

The fire trucks are here

We got everyone out

Someone called 911

I can't get it out

There's a fire

Madison shook so badly she almost dropped her phone. Staring blankly at the screen she tried to process what she was reading. A fire? Benny. She had to go. Sprinting back inside she ran straight into Ryan. He caught her and kept her upright.

"Oh my god. Madison, what's the matter? You're shivering."

"Benny," was all she could say. She handed her phone to Ryan.

He read through the messages. "Let's go. Did you bring anything?"

"There's a bin behind the bar. My purse and sweater are in it."

"I'll get them. Do you want to wait here in the entryway?"

Madison nodded. Numbly, she sat on a bench with her face in her hands. Ryan returned, holding her purse and handing her the sweater to put on.

"Chloe's coming too. She's talked Jesse into manning the bar. Jake said he'd help Dusty clean up."

"But…" Madison couldn't just leave.

"No buts. Jesse said he has some server certificate that's still valid from being a bartender. Whatever that means. Jake knows how to clean. Dusty knows what needs to be done and when."

"He was only a bartender for a month."

"Yes, but he's been drinking with me for years. He'll be fine." Chloe swept Madison up in a hug. "Is Benny okay? Is everyone okay?"

"I don't know. I'll message him that we are on the way."

The three of them piled into the bench seat of Madison's truck. Ryan took the wheel and Madison sat in the middle. She and Chloe curled into each other. Madison still shook, but Ryan couldn't tell if it was from being cold or from the shock. He pushed the lever for the heat over as far as it would go and turned the fan all the way up. He opened the vents that he could reach, and Chloe opened the ones on her side of the truck. The cab warmed quickly, but the windows also fogged up. Madison pulled a red bandana from the visor and wiped the condensation off the best she could.

"If you crack the window, it will help a little," Madison said.

Ryan cranked the window open an inch. Madison watched the little drips of rain coming in, hitting his arm until his shirt sleeve was soaked through. She reached across him and tried to dry him off. The red bandana was her dad's. He had tons of them. He kept them in the truck, in his back pocket to wipe the sweat off his face, and in his jacket pockets for when Madison's nose ran. The soft fabric was worn and faded from many washings. She twisted it in her hands, wishing that Ryan would drive faster, but knowing how dangerous that would be in the rain.

What had she done? She had cursed her life with the restaurant and now Benny said it was gone? What did he mean by gone?

When they pulled into the parking lot, there were several fire trucks. Lights flashed and floodlights illuminated everything. Madison gasped and Chloe started crying. Ryan tried to pull in, but a firefighter stopped him.

Ryan rolled the window down.

"You'll have to move on. We need room to do our work here."

Madison leaned over. "It's my café. I own the place."

"You're Madison?" he asked. "Okay. That cook has been asking for you. We'll need some information from you, too. You can park over there near the ambulance."

"Ambulance," Madison repeated.

Ryan pulled over to the far side of the parking lot, away from the fire crew. Chloe and Madison spilled out of the truck and ran over to the ambulance. Benny had a mask on but pulled it off when he saw them.

"I'm sorry, Madison. I tried to put it out, but it burned so fast." Benny started coughing.

"Mask on. Benjamin. We need to bring you in now."

"I'm so sorry. I tried."

Madison shook her head. "You don't have to be sorry Benny." She turned to the paramedic, who fastened the mask over Benny's face. "Is he going to be all right?"

"We have to get him in for evaluation. Smoke inhalation can be very dangerous." The paramedic disappeared into the ambulance with Benny, and they shut the doors. Madison, Ryan, and Chloe moved out of the way while the ambulance put on its siren and drove off.

They turned their attention to the café. Madison took one look at the blackened shell of a restaurant and fainted.

CHAPTER 20

Ryan caught Madison before she fell to the ground. A nearby firefighter took his jacket off and laid it on the ground. Gently, Ryan lowered her down.

"We need to get her feet elevated above her heart," he said, lifting her ankles to raise her legs.

Madison quickly came to. "What? What the hell?" She struggled to get up.

"Whoa, slow down there, ma'am. You need to sit up slowly."

"Like hell! My café!" Madison tried sitting up, but the spins overwhelmed her. She lay right back down. "Maybe I need a minute."

"Ma'am, are you feeling nauseous?"

"No."

"Are you feeling any pain?"

"No."

"When was the last time you had anything to eat or drink?"

"Um, I had some fries around three and a cola around five."

"All right now, you can start sitting up, slowly this time. Let's get her a bottle of water here." He called out and someone handed him a bottle. "You need to take better care of yourself. Here, take a sip."

Madison did as she was told. The firefighter slowly helped her stand up. Ryan offered her his arm and helped her over to the truck to sit in the cab.

"Are you okay? This is crazy." Chloe had tears in her eyes as she sat next to Madison.

"No. I want to leave. There's nothing I can do here."

"You two wait here. I'll be right back." Ryan walked over to a firefighter on the outskirts. He talked with him a moment and handed him something before walking back over to the truck.

"Let's get you out of here," Ryan said.

They piled back into the truck and headed into town.

As they pulled into the service club's parking lot, Ryan asked, "Chloe, are you okay to drive?" Tears still streamed down her cheeks, but her sobbing had quieted.

"Yeah, I'm fine. I'm going to the hospital to check on Benny."

"Poor Benny," Madison said softly. "I'll go with you."

"No way." Ryan stared at Madison. "You're going home, you're going to eat something and you're going to rest. If you won't let me help you, I'll go in and ask one of my cousins to take over."

"No. Don't do that. They're celebrating." Madison grabbed Chloe's hand. "You'll text me as soon as you hear something, right?"

"Of course." Chloe squeezed Madison's hand.

They all walked into the service club together. The party was over. The band was packing their equipment. Everyone had cleared out except Camille and Patricia, who were scurrying around packing what they needed to take with them. Chloe went over to help Jesse and Jake pack the bar.

When Dusty saw them, she stopped short. "What happened to you guys?"

Ryan watched Madison sink into a chair before she answered. "There was a fire. The restaurant is gone."

Dusty's eyes grew wide. "Are you serious? Did anyone get hurt?"

"Benny got everyone out. I know this is hard news for you, but I need to get Madison home. She's been through a lot today. Are you going to be okay?"

"Sure, I guess. It's so weird. Our café. Gone. I guess I'm not going in for my shift tomorrow."

Madison burst into tears.

"I'm sorry, Madison. I didn't mean anything." Dusty started crying too.

Madison stood to give her a hug. "It's not you. Let's have Jesse give you a ride home. Do you want me to let your parents know?"

"It's okay. They're waiting up for me. I'll talk to them when I get home."

Ryan walked over to Jake and Jesse. "Hey guys. Thanks for stepping in."

"How bad is it?" Jake asked.

"It's awful. I'm going to take Madison home. Can you guys give Dusty a ride home? And make sure Chloe is all right? She says she's going to the hospital to see Benny."

Jake gave him a nod. "You got it, bro. You all right?"

"I'm fine." Ryan half-hugged Jesse and clapped him on the back. "Thanks again for the help. I'll be in touch."

"Hey what should we do with all this stuff?" Jesse asked gestured to the bar and catering equipment. We can't bring it back to the restaurant."

"Oh right. I'll call Dad. Can you stick it in the garage at the cabin until I can figure something out?"

"Sure, but don't worry. I'll call him. You just take care of Madison. She looks dead on her feet." Jake nodded in Madison's direction.

Ryan walked over to her and held out his arm. "Are you ready?"

Madison nodded and took his arm.

Back in the truck, she turned the heat down. "It's making me sleepy," she said and leaned her head against the window. Before long she fell asleep anyway.

Despite everything, Ryan smiled fondly at her. Even caked in mud with tangled hair and a tear-stained face, he found her beautiful. His heart went out to her. Her entire day had been terrible, she was running on empty, and in the end she had comforted Dusty. She made sure the girl was taken care of before leaving.

She didn't wake up when he pulled into her driveway. He looked through her keys and took a guess at which one would open the door. He found the right one, opened the door and flicked on the lights before going back to the truck to wake her up. As gently as he could, he opened the truck door, ready to catch her if she fell out. She woke with a start.

"I fell asleep," she murmured.

"You sure did. Let's get you inside."

He put his arm around her, and she leaned in to him. He helped her through the doorway, and she walked slowly into the middle of the room.

"I'm exhausted."

"I'm sure you are. Do you want to get cleaned up?"

"Mm-hmm."

She shuffled over to the closet, took out a pajama set and then shuffled into the bathroom. He heard water running and worried about her showering in her state. She was so tired she could fall. He strained to listen for her while he rummaged through her refrigerator and cupboards. He found the makings for hot chocolate and warmed the milk. He put together a plate with some fruit, meat, and cheese. He had a feeling if he made a whole sandwich, she wouldn't even touch it. Maybe she would nibble on something before she fell back asleep.

She came out of the bathroom in her pajamas with her hair wrapped in a towel. She sat at the small table and sipped her hot chocolate.

"I'll never complain about hot cocoa, but I could sure use something stronger." Madison took a piece of cheese and started eating.

"I saw vodka in the cupboard. Do you want a splash?"

"I'd rather have the rum."

Ryan pulled the bottle out of the cupboard and added a splash to both of their mugs. He tentatively took a sip. "Not too bad."

"It will work."

They sat sipping their cocoa. Madison ate almost everything from the plate.

"Madison, I…"

"No. Not tonight. No talking about any of it tonight." She finished her cocoa and stood. She took her mug over to the sink and rinsed it out. She swayed on her feet.

"Into bed. I'll take care of it."

She didn't argue. She crawled under her covers and fell fast asleep. Ryan cleared the table and did the few dishes before turning the lights low. He plugged Madison's phone in to charge and made sure the sound was turned off. He pulled a blanket out of the basket and sunk into one of her cushioned chairs. He discovered it was a recliner and made himself comfortable. Soon he fell asleep as well.

He didn't sleep well. He kept jolting awake and checking on Madison. She slept fitfully, but she slept. He gave up and decided to get ready for the day. He searched her closet, found a T-shirt that would fit and took a shower. As quietly as possible, he made a pot of coffee and took a cup out onto the front porch. He left the entry door open enough to hear if Madison woke up.

At seven, her grandparents pulled into the driveway. Their faces were drawn and tired.

"Is she still sleeping? Did you spend the night here? Is she all right?" Madison's grandmother fired off questions.

"Yes ma'am. Yes, I slept on the chair. She was in shock, and I didn't want to leave her."

"That's good. We'll stop by again later then. Give us a call when she's awake, will you?"

"Yes ma'am."

"It's Mabel. And this is Donald."

"Call me Don." He shook Ryan's hand. "How do you do?"

Ryan smiled wryly. "Pleased to meet you."

"Here then." Mabel handed Ryan a basket. "It's her favorite, strawberry rhubarb muffins."

"Thank you, Mabel. I'll have her call you as soon as she wakes up. Here." He set the muffins on a table and pulled out his wallet. "My business card has my cell on it if you need anything."

Mabel tucked the card into her pocket. She gave Ryan a quick hug, and then said goodbye. Ryan wondered if he should have had them stay. Surely Madison would rather have them around to take care of her. It was too late now. They had already left. He figured he would call them later if she kicked him out.

The texts and phone calls started coming in from his family. He answered them as best he could but didn't have much information to give them. Madison would have to contact the liaison at the fire department during business hours tomorrow. Until they gave her an all clear, she couldn't even enter what was left of the building.

At noon, Madison hadn't gotten out of bed. Ryan went inside to check on her. She lay curled up tight while she slept. She had fallen asleep with her towel wrapped around her head, but her hair had freed itself during the night. Her hair spilled wild over the pillowcase. Gently, he rubbed her arm and quietly said her name. Her long lashes betrayed her squinting eyes. She took her time in opening them.

"You're still here?"

"Do you want me to go?"

Madison didn't answer right away. She stared blankly at the far wall. Then, with a small smile, she answered him. "No, I'm glad you stayed. I don't want to be alone right now."

"Then I won't leave you."

Madison avoided his gaze. A blush crept over her cheeks. "Where did you sleep?"

"In one of your chairs. I don't know if I'd call it sleep, though," Ryan said and chuckled.

'Oh, I can make some coffee." Madison moved to get up.

"I'll do it. Your grandparents were here and dropped off muffins. If you want, I can make you an omelet to go with them."

"An omelet sounds delicious. My grandparents dropped off muffins?"

"You're supposed to call them when you wake up."

Madison reached for her phone. Her face fell when she saw all the missed calls and messages.

"Don't worry about them. Call who you need to call, and we'll worry about responding to everyone else later. My phone has stopped buzzing if you'd rather use it to make your calls."

"Sure." Great big teardrops raced down Madison's face.

Ryan sat next to her on the bed. He put his arm around her, and she leaned in to him.

"It doesn't even feel real. I feel like I should be there working, serving the lunch crowd."

"I'm sure it will feel strange for a while. You will still feel different after you rebuild, but everything will be okay. You'll be okay." He wiped away the tears streaming down her cheeks with his thumb.

Madison lifted her face and kissed him. It was a soft, sweet kiss that melted his heart. She pulled away and went to her closet to find clothes for the day. Ryan didn't know what to think. He received such mixed messages from Madison. He wanted to take care of her, but he didn't want to take advantage of the situation.

They would have to talk about their problems, but for now, he wanted to make sure she ate something before the day overwhelmed her.

He cooked while Madison fixed her hair and dressed. He had the first omelet ready by the time she emerged from the bathroom. She wore baggy jean shorts and a gigantic t-shirt with a sunflower on it. She had tamed her hair into a messy bun. The tears had been scrubbed from her face, leaving her skin pink. She joined him in the tiny kitchen and fixed her coffee.

"Where are the muffins?"

"On the table already."

She settled into a chair at the table with a leg tucked under her. She scrolled through messages and ignored the incoming calls. Ryan added a plate of fruit to the table and joined her to eat.

"I texted my grandparents. They invited us for supper." She added shyly, "if you want to join us."

"I'd love to."

"Chloe says Benny is still coughing. They want to keep him until tomorrow morning, but he's being a grouch. She went home to shower and change before she goes back there. I want to go see him, too. Maybe he can tell me what happened last night."

"The firefighter I spoke to when we left said they thought it was lightning, but it could take time to find out. I hope Benny is okay. My family sends their sympathies. No one can really believe it."

"I can't either. I feel so numb."

They both reached for the same muffin on the plate. Ryan let Madison have it.

Madison began to tear up again. "Gladys says she and her dog, Jameson, are sorry to hear about the fire. She promises she'll be back as soon as we rebuild. The fishermen send their condolences and want to know if they can help. Dylan said his crew will be available when we're ready to rebuild." The tears streamed down her face. "All of the staff are saying they'll come back when we reopen. What are they going to do in the meantime?"

Ryan reached across the table and took her hand. He gave it a squeeze. "Put the phone down. Take some deep breaths. We'll get to all that. We'll get your staff taken care of. I promise." He knew whatever it took, he would see Madison through this.

CHAPTER 21

Madison didn't have an appetite, but Ryan kept encouraging her until she ate her whole meal. It all tasted like sawdust, even her Grandma Mabel's homemade muffins. She wanted to crawl back into bed and pull the covers over her head. Exhaustion still overwhelmed her, but she had to get moving.

She had to check on Benny. She wanted to see the restaurant in the daylight. She needed to check on her employees. Her phone still vibrated with messages and phone calls.

They took a few minutes to clean the dishes together. Madison washed while Ryan dried. She was glad to have a small task to concentrate on. She made her bed and tidied the cabin, wanting a clean, calm space when she came home.

Ryan pulled up directions to the hospital so she wouldn't have to talk if she didn't want to. Sitting in the middle of the bucket seat she laid her head on his shoulder. She stared through the window at the road without really seeing anything.

Madison didn't know what to expect when they arrived at the hospital. When they stepped off the elevator, she heard someone call her name. She barely had time to turn when Chloe bulldozed into her with a hug. She had been in the waiting room with two of Benny's sisters.

"I'm so glad you're here. Benny will be happy to see you. I keep telling him it wasn't his fault, but he feels so guilty he couldn't put the fire out."

"It wasn't his fault at all. They think it might have been lightning. Can I see him?"

"They're only letting a few of us in at a time and they're kicking us out when he falls asleep. Which is a lot. We can go and poke our heads in. He's been asking for you and his sisters have been in there awhile."

Ryan stayed behind in the waiting room. Chloe held Madison's hand and wouldn't stop talking.

"He looks so weird in a hospital gown. I'm so glad his burns are minor. They were worried he burned his throat, but it's the smoke and I guess toxins. He's probably okay, but they have him on oxygen to help clear out his system. They tried to have a mask on him, but he kept pulling it off. They gave in and let him have those nose tube things."

Chloe knocked on the door. "In case he's in the bathroom or something," she whispered. "I don't need to see his backside as he gets into bed. Do you think they let him wear underwear?" She opened the door.

His oldest sister, Heather, patted Benny's feet. "We'll let these crazy kids have a turn with you. We'll be back."

"Madison. You're here." Benny started coughing.

"I had to see you. I've been so worried about you." Madison took the chair closest to Benny. When his coughing let up, she grabbed his hand.

"I'm all right. They're just making sure. I didn't get burned too bad. I have a good burn here on my arm, though." He lifted his other arm to show her the bandage. "Hey, if you want a hot bod, I don't recommend using fire."

"I'll remember that one," Madison said.

"Very funny, Benny. You could have been really hurt. What the heck were you thinking? Leah said you went back in after you got everyone out." Chloe had her arms crossed and a dark look on her face.

"I went in to put the fire out. Hey, I saw this and shoved it in my apron pocket." Benny rolled onto his side and grabbed for his bed tray. He handed her the picture of her parents. The glass was broken, but the picture was fine. "Anyway, I thought with the sprinklers on I could put the rest of it out with the fire extinguishers. I didn't realize how fast it spread."

Madison sat there holding onto the picture while another waterfall of tears wet her cheeks. "Benny, I don't know what to say. You could have died."

This time Benny took Madison's hand. "You can't be scared of dying. People die all the time, and you don't hear them complaining about it."

Chloe stood and stamped her foot. "You are impossible. How can you joke at a time like this?"

Benny started coughing.

"Are you coughing so I won't yell at you?"

Benny shook his head no.

A nurse came into the room. "Benny has another test to do and afterwards he will need to rest. Are you ready, Benny?"

"I have a question first."

"I'll try to answer it, but we may need to wait for the doctor."

"If smoking kills people and bacon kills people, how come smoked bacon is cured?"

The nurse looked like she wanted to scold Benny, but a smile slowly broke across her face, and she laughed. "You'll definitely have to ask the doctor about that."

Chloe was not amused. "One of these days, Benny. One of these days." She turned and flounced out of the room as if he'd deeply insulted her.

Madison couldn't help herself and giggled. "I think you're going to make it, my friend. I'll visit again soon." She followed Chloe back to the waiting room. Chloe told Benny's sisters about her plans. She told them she planned to head out and would see Benny when he went home. Madison knew Chloe wanted to yell at him without witnesses.

Ryan pushed the button for the elevator. Chloe stood there, tapping her foot. Madison looked at her picture and tears welled up again.

Madison handed Ryan the picture. "It's my parents at the café. When they first took it over. Benny grabbed it when he tried to fight the fire."

"Idiot," Chloe muttered under her breath.

They all stepped into the elevator.

"Chloe, are you all right?" Madison put her arm around her friend.

"No." The tears spilled down Chloe's face. "Benny and I had a huge fight. He said I should quit dating losers, and I deserved better. I told him to mind his own business, because at least I go on dates. Then he almost got himself killed in this stupid fire. And we should all be at work right now, but there is no work.

And we're here in this stupid hospital elevator and this place smells of bad rubbing alcohol and sick people."

Madison pulled her friend into a hug. "Benny is fine. We are fine. That's a good start. I'll figure something out. I need a little time to get my bearings."

The elevator opened, and Madison let Chloe go.

"I'll be okay. I just need a break. I'm going to head home." Chloe sniffed and wiped the tears off her cheeks.

"I'll call you later," Madison assured her.

"Not if I call you first," Chloe said with a little wave.

Madison let Ryan drive again.

"Where to?" he asked her.

"I guess the grocery store. If I can't eat at work, I'll need more food at the house."

Madison pointed out the grocery store sign a few blocks up the street. She hoped it wouldn't be busy. Sunday afternoon seemed like a quiet time to go through and buy what she needed.

They went inside and Madison filled the cart with her fruits and vegetables.

"Madison!" It was Jessica, from the book club. Madison tried not to cringe. Jessica came right up to her and gave her a hug. "I heard about the café. It's terrible news. Is everyone safe and sound?"

"Benny is in the hospital, but I think he'll be okay. Everyone else is fine."

"It's a wonder no one was hurt in such a huge fire. What happened?"

"They think maybe lightning. They'll let me know."

Ryan stepped in between them. "I'm sorry to cut this short, but we'll have to get going. Can Madison catch up with you later when she knows more about what happened?"

"Of course. Do keep in touch, Madison. The CLSLC is here for you if you need anything."

"Thank you. I appreciate it." Madison smiled feebly.

They were stopped several times as they made their way through the market. Madison marveled at how well Ryan took care of people. He was polite but firm with everyone who stopped them.

Madison wasn't sure what she was doing. She relied on Ryan even though she hardly knew him. Part of her wanted to send him on his way, but the rest of her was relieved he was there. Carefully and thoughtfully, he took care of her when she wanted to collapse into a puddle. It felt strange to rely on him. Her heart swirled with a million feelings about him, but for right now, she was grateful he stood by her side.

They loaded the groceries into the back of the truck. Madison wanted to see the restaurant, but she couldn't face it.

"Let's head back to my place. I need to get these groceries put away before my ice cream melts."

"Good idea."

Madison sat by the window. She wanted to sit in the middle and curl up next to Ryan again, but it felt awkward. Instead, she sat silently with her hands in her lap as she stared out the window. She watched the fields full of wheat and the belts of trees pass them by. Most of the time, the scenery filled her heart with contentment. Today, it passed by in a blur.

"Oh, wow."

Ryan's voice pulled Madison out of her daze. They had pulled into her driveway. Chloe sat on her front porch surrounded by casserole dishes, baked goods, and flowers.

Madison forgot about all of the groceries. "What is all of this?"

Chloe gave her a wry smile. "People keep dropping off food. I guess they're worried you'll go hungry." Chloe raised an eyebrow at Ryan, who had his hands full of grocery bags. "You aren't going to need groceries."

"What am I going to do with all of this? My fridge is tiny."

"Hm, maybe use the house fridge?" Chloe asked with a shrug.

"Right. The house fridge."

"What do you want where?" Ryan asked.

"I guess put the groceries in here. We can put the casseroles in the house freezer. We can ask if any of the employees need them. I think I'll get rid of the baked goods, too. If I eat all of them, I'll end up gaining a ton of weight."

"You're not going to throw them out, are you?" Chloe's eyes grew wide.

"I'm going to drop some off at the firehouse. I'll see if the day camp program wants any. Maybe the employees will take the rest. Oh, is that a lake cake?"

"It sure is," Chloe said.

"What's a lake cake?" Ryan asked.

"It's a blueberry, lemon, cheesecake masterpiece. Who made it?" Madison asked Chloe.

"Amy. Dylan dropped it off a few minutes ago. He said to tell you whenever you are ready to build, his crew is ready for you."

"I think I met Dylan at the café. Is Amy his wife?" Ryan asked.

"She is. She's also the best baker in the county. I'm keeping the cake."

Ryan shifted on his feet. He still held the grocery bags. Madison picked up the lake cake and opened the door for him. Together, Ryan and Madison put the groceries away. Chloe caught Madison's eye and made a face at her, asking about Ryan without exchanging any words. Madison shrugged and managed a small smile.

The three of them gathered the casseroles and headed over to the main house. Madison unlocked the door and led them to the kitchen. Stifling heat poured out of the house.

"It's like an oven in here," Chloe complained.

"I heat it in the winter, so the pipes don't freeze, but I don't bother cooling it off in the summer. I just open the windows when I come over to clean."

"That makes sense," Ryan said. "This place is incredible. How old is it?"

Madison talked as she organized the food. "They built the house in 1912, before the war. The guest cabin was built after the war in 1921. There were some outbuildings, too, but they were torn down. I'm not sure when. A single garage was built sometime in the fifties. They tore it down in the early eighties, built the two-stall garage and attached it to the house with the mudroom-slash-laundry room." Madison put the last of the casseroles in the freezer. "This place has been in our family the whole time."

"I've never been in here," Chloe said, looking around.

Madison paused. "I only come in here to clean. I guess sometimes if I want an actual bath, too. The cabin only has the shower."

"I wish I could have the bathroom long enough to take a bath. I can barely get a shower in without one of my brothers pounding on the door."

"You can always move out," Madison said.

"You see, the thing is, I don't currently have a job." Chloe stared at the floor.

"Damn. I need to figure this out. I can't leave everyone hanging." Madison locked the door, and they walked back over to the cabin.

"I need to see it. I need to get over there."

Ryan opened the truck door for her.

"I'll ride with you two," Chloe said quietly.

Madison hugged Chloe before she climbed into the truck.

"Let's do this," Madison said, squaring her shoulders and giving a nod. "I'm ready."

CHAPTER 22

Ryan could see the weight of the stress that Madison carried. He could see the enormous effort it took her to put one foot in front of the other. He wanted to tell her to slow down and rest, but he knew she wouldn't be able to. She would keep going until she crashed again.

He watched Madison and Chloe. They were standing silent and holding on to each other. They stared at the black, jagged wreck of a building. The smiles and bright sunshine that had filled the building were gone, even though the sun shone brightly. Everyone felt cold and cloudy. Ryan didn't know what to do for them, so he stood off to the side and let them grieve.

Madison made a move. She grabbed a rock from the side of the parking lot and heaved it at the café. It hit a windowpane with a crash.

"Nice aim," Chloe said. "Want to go to The Corner?"

"What about dinner with your grandparents?" Ryan did not want to bring them out drinking. It seemed like a terrible idea.

"I can't handle it, sitting there listening to them pity me. Again. I'll text them so they won't worry."

Ryan eyed her warily.

"If you don't want to go, I can drop you off."

"I have a feeling you two are going to need a DD. If you want me to go with, I'll go."

Madison answered him with a nod.

Against his better judgement, they all piled back into the pickup to go.

True to her word, Madison texted her grandparents. Ryan didn't know what she said to them, but they texted back and forth almost the whole way to the bar. He stole glances at her, but her face was unreadable, as if she had turned to stone.

There were no open spots in the parking lot of The Corner. He dropped Madison and Chloe off at the front door and drove around. He ended up parking in the grass next to a long line of vehicles.

Once he entered the bar, he had to wade through a sea of people. He made his way to the back of the bar where he found a tight ball of people hugging and crying. He couldn't see her, but he knew Madison was in the middle of them all. Staff, friends, and the community surrounded her.

The tables were littered with drink cups and beer cans, but he didn't see much food. He grabbed a passing server and ordered nachos and several pizzas along with a club soda. There was no way he was going to drink tonight. Someone needed to stay sober.

He noticed his brother at a table off to the side. He and Jesse had a pitcher in front of them, but they were drinking sodas. Pulling up a chair, he joined them at the table.

"A pitcher of car keys?" he asked.

"No one drives home drunk tonight. We have a few sober drivers lined up if they're needed." Jesse answered.

"That's genius. I ordered some food. Maybe if they eat something they won't get too crazy," Ryan said.

"Good call." Jake clapped a hand on Ryan's shoulder. "The bartenders aren't serving shots tonight either, just in case."

Ryan glanced over his shoulder at Madison. The crowd seemed to give her strength. She had needed to see her people today as much as they needed to see her.

Pulling out his cell phone, Ryan sent off a text to his boss.

I'm in a situation here and I won't make it back to the city for a few days. We'll have to get together for lunch some other time.

Jake and Jesse were discussing game system specs. Ryan wasn't into it so he scrolled through his email. An email from his mother caught his eye.

"Damn it," he muttered.

"What's wrong, bro?"

"I forgot to call mom. I'm going to head outside so I can hear her," Ryan answered.

Outside wasn't much quieter. On the far edge of the parking lot, he leaned against a tree and read her email.

Ryan – It's rude to say you'll call and then neglect to do so. I understand you may be busy, but a few minutes for your mother doesn't seem too much to ask. Are you still at Cloud Lake? Do I need to come out there? Call me! XOXO Laura Covington

He rarely allowed himself the luxury, but Ryan rolled his eyes. He ran his fingers through his hair, put on a brilliant smile, and called his mother.

The few minutes of his time turned into an hour. Ryan found himself telling her everything about Madison, his dad, the resort, his plans, the party, and the fire.

"Ryan, if anyone else told me all of this, I would say they were making up stories. Do you realize how ludicrous this all sounds?"

"I can hardly believe it myself."

"Hmm, and this Madison. You seem to have gotten close fairly quickly."

"Yes, we have."

"Hmm."

"Mom, you need to stop hmm-ing at me. A lot has gone wrong, but there's potential here. I'm tired of living the life Dad laid out for me."

"He meant well."

Ryan didn't know what to say to that. "Right. Well. I have to get back inside."

"Very well. Keep in touch. I love you."

"I love you, too." They hung up and he stared at his phone screen.

"You love who?" Madison demanded to know.

Ryan looked up to see Madison standing in front of him. Their eyes met. Intense feelings of desire washed over him. He swallowed hard.

"My mother." Trying to head off any chance of a fight, he held out his phone to show her: 1h 4m 11s Laura Covington.

"Your mom's name is Laura Covington?"

"It is now. It used to be Laura Davis when she married my dad but changed it back to Laura Covington after the divorce."

"Huh. I need my keys." Madison swayed on her feet. The lack of shots didn't matter. She'd managed to get wasted without them.

"Hey, beautiful." Ryan flashed a smile at her.

"What?" Her voice had a twinge of belligerence.

"Can I give you a ride?"

"You called me beautiful."

"And I meant it."

Madison looked tense as she tried hard to understand that thought. She soon gave up. "Okay."

Ryan deposited Madison in the truck before he texted his brother.

I'm taking Madison home. Is Chloe ready to go?

Chloe says she's not going anywhere and to bring Madison back

Not happening

We'll get Chloe home later

Thanks

"Who are you texting?" Madison's voice had an edge to it.

"My brother. I'm making sure Chloe is okay."

"We should go get her."

"She'll come along later. To get her car. You can see her when she picks it up."

"Oh good."

Madison drunk seemed stormy. Ryan couldn't tell if her mood would dissipate or let loose. The ride home was quiet at first. Madison sat holding her purse in her lap and stared out the side window.

"I'm not drunk." Madison's words slurred.

"I didn't think so."

"Maybe."

"Maybe you're not drunk? You were only in there an hour."

"Yes! And I only had three straws!"

"Straws? In your drinks?"

"I kept my straws," she insisted.

"Do you mean you had three drinks?"

"Mm-hmm. Three Cloud Lakes."

Ryan's grip tightened on the wheel. "They serve Cloud Lakes at the bar?"

"Yup, your cousin said it makes you forget everything."

"Let me guess. Patty?"

"Yes! I just love her!"

Ryan groaned and Madison fell silent again. Three Cloud Lake teas seemed like a lot, but Madison was still upright. Maybe she would be fine.

"I didn't get any pizza."

"Do you want pizza? I can have one brought out for you."

"No."

"Are you hungry?"

"I don't know."

They arrived at her cabin. The sun had lowered, but the light still shone over the tree line. The front gardens glowed in the last rays of day. The diffused sunbeams seemed to set the blooms on fire. Madison threw her purse on the seat and jumped out of the truck before Ryan could even put it in park.

Madison ran to a planter and stuck her face in the flowers. Concerned she was getting sick, Ryan ran over to help her. He heard her taking in deep breaths. She raised her head, beaming.

"I love my flowers." Her smile was radiant.

"They're wonderful. Are you good with your flowers for a moment?"

Madison didn't answer but stuck her face into another nearby planter. Ryan took it as a yes and went into her cabin. He found a small basket on top of her cupboards and filled it. Small containers of fruits, nuts, cheeses and crackers went into it, and he added a few sodas. Digging through her stash of blankets, he found one that looked like it could be used outside. He pulled it out of the pile, grabbed the basket and went to find her.

She wasn't in the front with her face in the flowers. He went around to her back patio and didn't see her there, either. Following the path behind the garage, he passed the main house and walked through the rest of the gardens. He found Madison standing on a small beach by the lake.

"I have a picnic. May I join you?"

"Yes, you may."

Ryan handed Madison the basket and spread the blanket out on the sand. He took the basket from her and set it on the edge. They sank to the ground and Madison leaned against him. She fed him a strawberry.

While they ate, they watched the small waves roll onto shore. In the distance, they heard the laughing call of a loon. Soon after, another loon answered back. The sun lit up the trees on the opposite shore into brilliant greens.

"I think my limit is two Cloud drinks," she said and took a sip of her soda.

"They are pretty potent."

"Not potent enough. I didn't forget."

Ryan smoothed a strand of her hair. "I don't think it's possible, not with tragedies this big. It's going to take time to grieve."

"I don't know what I'm going to do tomorrow."

"We'll have to take it one step at a time."

"Are you sure you want to stick around? My life is a disaster." Ryan's heart went out to her. He knew he wasn't responsible for any of it, but he wanted to fix it all for her. He wanted to see her eyes light up like when they first met. He missed her grin and good-natured chatter.

"As long as you'll let me. I'm here for you, Madison."

She lifted her face towards him. Madison kissed him with sugary-sweet lips that tasted of strawberries and cola. Pulling away, she gazed at him with a serious face.

"Want to go to bed?"

Ryan knew that was a very bad idea.

"I mean I'm tired. Are you staying over? Will you?" Her eyes pled with him, and he wrestled with his conscience. She seemed to be sobering up enough, but he didn't want to leave her.

He smiled at her and nodded. "I'll stay over."

They packed what was left of their picnic into the basket and walked together through the gardens to her cabin. Twilight descended. The air cooled as the sun sunk behind the trees. They were serenaded by the sounds of nature – crickets chirped, frogs croaked, and the gentle breeze rustled the leaves. The evening was peaceful.

Inside, Ryan unpacked the basket and washed the few dishes. Madison disappeared into the closet and rummaged around. She emerged with two sets of pajama pants and t-shirts. She handed him gray plaid pants and a soft gray t-shirt. Ryan didn't ask where they came from. He was happy to get out of the shorts he'd been wearing for the past few days.

"Chloe left them here."

"The pajamas?"

"Yep, we had a sleepover and she wore them. I think she swiped them from her little brother."

"How big is her little brother?" Ryan held up the pajama pants. They would be long on him.

"A little taller than you." Madison shrugged and went to change into her pajamas. They were bright pink with tiny red hearts all over them.

After she emerged from the bathroom, ready for bed, he went in to change. When he came out, Madison was already lying in her bed. He'd planned on sleeping in the chair again, but she had left the covers down for him.

"I'm good with the chair." Ryan knew she was still tipsy and overtired.

"Please," she said. Her soft voice pleaded with him. "Will you sleep with me tonight?"

A war raged inside of him, but he was too tired to fight. Giving in, he slid under the covers next to her. She curled into his chest, and he put his arm around her. It didn't take long for her to fall asleep. It took Ryan much longer. Her hair still smelled faintly of her strawberry conditioner. He could feel her chest rise and fall with every breath. She fit perfectly against him, as if they belonged together. It took a lot of willpower and concentration to stay calm and fall asleep.

CHAPTER 23

Madison woke to moonlight streaming through the window. Ryan curled around her, and she lay wrapped in his arms. Her mouth was dry, and she wondered what time it was. She needed something to drink but couldn't figure out how to crawl over him without waking him up.

He murmured in her ear, "Would you like a glass of water?"

Electricity crackled through her. She whispered, "Yes, please."

Madison watched him enter the kitchen. They had been spending so much time together, he knew which cupboard she kept the glasses in. He hadn't even turned on a light. She pulled her gaze from him to check the time. Her phone read 4:44. If this were a normal day, she would be getting up soon to get ready for work.

Today there was no reason to get out of bed, but there was plenty of reason to stay in. Ryan handed her a cool glass of water, and she drank greedily. He too had a glass of water. She paused to watch him. In the moonlight, she could see the motion of his throat as he swallowed. She wanted to kiss him there. She set her glass on the nightstand and moved over, giving him room to get back into bed with her.

He lay next to her. She could barely see him in the shadows of the night, but she could feel him. Softly, she ran a hand up and down his arm. She heard him inhale, but he didn't stop her. The air in the cabin was cool, but she burned with wanting him. The quiet of the night gave her confidence. She slipped her hand under his shirt so she could explore his hard stomach. His breath caught again as her arm moved up to his chest. She remembered the morning she'd seen him in the sun, glistening and golden.

Her lips found his in the darkness. Tentatively, she kissed him. He brought a hand to her face, caressing her. Her kisses became more demanding, and he answered them with urgency. His hand moved into her hair and tugged. She took a moment to catch her breath and turned towards him to kiss him more deeply. She wanted more. Trailing kisses along his throat, she heard him groan.

"Madison, slow down," he pleaded with her.

She licked at his throat and moved so she could look into his eyes. Even in the dim moonlight she could see his eyes darken. He wanted her, too. She waited for him to say something. He didn't seem to know what to say.

Madison knew what she wanted, and she was blunt about it. "I want you," she whispered.

He closed his eyes tight, then slowly opened them. "I want you too, but I can wait. I don't want you to regret anything."

"Life is too short for regrets."

He seemed to search her eyes before replying. "Are you sure?"

She smiled. "Absolutely."

He groaned and took her into his arms. His kisses ignited fires inside of her. Their hands pulled at each other's clothes, impatient to be rid of them. A flicker of a thought that this was too good to be true entered Madison's mind, but she banished it and let her passion guide her. Life truly was too short for regrets.

Afterwards, they lay tangled. The sun streamed into the cabin. Madison knew she should get moving and start the day, but she couldn't resist lying naked in Ryan's arms. Strong and muscular, she loved having his arms around her. She started caressing one at the thought.

This time when he groaned, it was followed by a laugh. "Have mercy on me, Madison. I'm only a man."

"I noticed," she said with a soft hum.

"Did you just purr?"

"I think I did. Want to see if you can make me do it again?"

He kissed her on the nose. "How about some coffee? And you have that nice bread, I could make French toast. Do you have syrup?"

"If I tell you where to go with my syrup, would you?"

He growled and climbed on top of her. He pinned her hands to the mattress and covered her with kisses. "You're insatiable."

She laughed and pushed him off of her. "All right, coffee and French toast. I'm going to take a shower."

She pulled out clean clothes and stopped. Madison turned to look at Ryan, feeling shy. Her confidence faltered, but she had to ask him. "Do you want to go get your things after breakfast? Or…"

He smiled at her. "I could use some clean clothes and I should get my SUV."

Relief washed over Madison. She knew he had to get back to the city, but she didn't want him to leave. He'd been such a comfort the past few days. She couldn't have gotten through them alone.

He rummaged through the kitchen, and she headed into the shower. She tried to concentrate on what she had to do today. She had to see what the fire department had to say. The memory of Ryan's kisses interrupted her train of thought. No, she had to concentrate.

She had to figure out how to help her employees. Why was she thinking of his hands on her body? They had to pick up Ryan's suitcase. Madison was about to start quivering at the thought of him.

She turned the water over to cold and hoped it would do the trick. It was one thing to give in to their desires in the moonlight and quiet of the early morning, but now she had to face the day. Her to-do list threatened to overwhelm her.

Stepping out of the shower, she dried herself off. After she dressed, she ran a brush through her hair. The smell of coffee called to her, and she couldn't wait to get her mug. She walked into the kitchen and wrapped her arms around Ryan, laying her head against his back.

He turned around and hugged her. Secure in his arms, she relaxed. He took his time before releasing her. She tried to move to his side to grab her coffee cup, but he didn't let her. She looked at him surprised at his serious expression.

"Is something wrong? Please tell me there's nothing. I can't take anything else right now."

"I have to go back to the city. There's trouble at work."

"Oh." Madison's face fell. "I see."

They heard a car pull up outside. A moment later, there was a knock at the door. Madison opened it to find Chloe.

"Good morning!" Chloe was too full of sunshine and smiles. Madison was tempted to shut the door on her.

Chloe breezed into the room. "I hope I'm not interrupting anything."

Madison slid her eyes over to Ryan and shook her head. "No, we were going to have breakfast. Are you joining us?"

Chloe shrugged. "If you insist. Is there still coffee?"

"How are you so chipper this morning?" Madison asked while she poured Chloe's coffee.

"I'm resilient, I guess. And I slept well. And Benny is getting released as soon as the doctor sees him." Chloe handed Ryan his keys. "I stayed at the resort last night. Molly sent your luggage, too. It's in your car."

"You brought my car over? Thanks!"

"I had to. My jeep is still here, remember? I wasn't about to walk ten miles."

"Still, I appreciate it." His eyes caught Madison's. "Is it all right if I grab a quick shower?"

Madison nodded. Ryan went out to get a fresh set of clothes.

"We were making French toast. Are you hungry?" Madison asked.

"Sounds good, but I have some questions."

"Like what?"

"Like why Ryan is here so early in the morning wearing my brother's pajamas. He does look cute in them and all, but…"

Chloe didn't finish her thought. Ryan came back in with his clothes and Chloe fell silent. Madison stared into her coffee cup. Ryan didn't seem to notice the tension.

He left the room and Madison spoke softly, "He's been spending the night. The first night he slept in the chair and last night I let him sleep with me. And you left the pajamas when we stayed up half the night watching movies last winter."

Chloe watched Madison flip the French toast. "I see."

Madison pulled out the syrup, peanut butter, and butter and handed them to Chloe. After Chloe placed them on the table, Madison handed her orange juice, glasses, and a bowl of fruit.

Chloe laughed. "Are you making sure I can still waitress when we go back to work?"

Madison groaned. "It's going to take forever to rebuild."

"They offered me a job at The Corner last night."

"Did you take it?"

"I said I'd let them know."

Madison handed Chloe a plate of French toast.

Ryan entered the room. "I hate to run out on you, but I have to get going. I'll call you later." He kissed Madison on the cheek and then he left. Madison burst into tears.

"Oh, my stars, you slept with him! What were you thinking?"

Madison turned off the stove and sat at the table. It took a moment to compose herself. "I don't know. He's been so nice to me, and he stayed when everything fell apart. Or so I thought, but he's as bad as the rest of them. He's running."

Chloe stared at Madison. "Are you serious right now? I thought he left to run an errand or something."

"No, there's something wrong where he works. He left to go back to the city."

"But he quit."

Madison started crying again. Her heart ached. This was too much. "I feel so lost."

Chloe grabbed Madison's hands. "I'm here for you. I'm always here for you. Life sucks right now, but we're going to get through this."

Madison managed a smile. "I haven't cried this much in ages."

"Maybe you should have. We'll get into that later. For now, let's finish breakfast and get to work. What's first on the list?"

"Contacting the fire department. I need to find out when I can get in there. I need to get a hold of insurance and figure out what they need. I need to call Dylan and plan a rebuild. I want to check on Benny. I need to check on the employees."

"Whoa. Slow down. We're doing one thing at a time. The list is big enough for now. We'll get through this. Later we will talk about this Ryan dilemma. When you're ready."

"I don't need to talk about that one. I don't know what I thought, but I see things clearly now. I knew he would be a mistake from the beginning."

Chloe's normally expressive face took on an unreadable expression.

Madison narrowed her eyes. "I did. I knew he'd desert me like everyone else."

Chloe reached across the table to take Madison's hand. Her face softened and in a calm voice she addressed her friend. "Madison, Ryan is not Jonah. He is not the summer fun boys that run through here. He's been at your side for days seeing you through this. Did you see his face as he was leaving? He looked miserable. Obviously he didn't want to leave."

"They all leave." Madison wasn't ready to hear what Chloe was saying to her.

Chloe ignored her. "Let's divide and conquer. I'll call employees while you call the fire department. What do you want me to say?"

"I did want to check on them myself, but maybe you're right. Let them know I will reach out to them later when I'm not so swamped. I've been thinking about it. I'm able to float everyone for two weeks. I wish I could do longer, but I don't know much about the insurance part of it. They can expect their paychecks for the next few weeks."

"That's generous of you, Madison. No one is expecting anything. You don't have to keep paying them."

"Business was good, and I can afford to do that much. A few weeks of pay is the least I can do for them. I want to help them find jobs, but I'm not sure how to help them right now. Maybe tell them to get a hold of me if they aren't finding anything."

"That's good. I'm sure we'll all dig up something."

"I want to ask them if they'll come back, but I don't know how to do it."

"Leave it to me. I'll get them talking and see what they're planning."

"Thank you. I can't think of anything else right now. I don't know when we're going to rebuild. I don't know anything."

"It's fine. You're doing the best you can."

"I'm trying." Madison stood up and grabbed their coffee cups. She refilled them and sat back down to start her calls.

CHAPTER 24

The drive home took four hours, but it seemed longer to Ryan. A cloud of misery spoiled his entire trip. He'd made a mistake leaving Madison behind. Especially after last night. He wanted to turn around, sweep Madison into his arms, kiss away her tears, and make love to her for days.

He never should have made love to her. He had wanted her badly, but he knew she felt vulnerable right now. When those hands of her started caressing him, it took all of his concentration to lie still. There had been no chance of behaving when she was so sure of herself. Absolutely, he had lost his mind and had taken advantage of her.

The road seemed endless, dragging on and on. He couldn't believe he left her. This was not good. How do you leave someone in their darkest moments and make it up to them? He wounded her when he said he had to go.

Chloe showing up had been a good thing and he was glad she did. Not from the convenience of getting his car back, but because he didn't like the thought of Madison being alone. She had a lot to deal with. He should be there for her, helping her move forward. At least Chloe could step in.

Ryan's phone rang, but he ignored it. It wasn't Madison's number, it was work. He refused to work from the road. The call ended and came through again. He silenced his phone. He would have to stop for gas before entering the suburbs. The messages could wait until then.

His last business deal was signed, sealed, and delivered. This would have to be someone else's mess, and he wasn't eager to clean it up. His last week should have been a walk in the park. He should have been able to coast through until the end, or at least he should have been able to take care of things from the lake.

His boss had texted while Madison was getting ready.

Unfortunately, we need you here. We have a crisis. I hate to mention it, but your severance depends on the terms of your notice being fulfilled.

Ryan's hands were tied. He needed that severance. He shouldn't have, but he had counted on the extra capital as part of his plans. Without it, he might have to take on a business partner for the winery.

He stopped in the suburbs to gas up his SUV. He sent Madison a text.

Almost back to the cities. How are you doing?

Madison didn't respond.

He checked his other messages. His boss had sent him a text.

Let me know when you will arrive. I'd prefer to meet in the boardroom instead of the restaurant. I'll have someone pick up lunch.

That didn't sound like a crisis to Ryan, but he messaged his boss an estimated arrival time.

He found a message from another agent. The guy managed to break his leg playing golf at the country club. He wondered if Ryan could take care of his clients for a few days. Another email said the CAPEH Group was on the lookout for a bigger building. The startup had outgrown their current space and was desperate for more. He had worked with them previously, but he would have to pass them off this time. There was no way they could close out a deal in the few days he had left at work.

Ryan glanced at his other emails but didn't see anything out of the ordinary. There was nothing pressing or flagged as urgent. Everything seemed to be business as usual.

It took him longer than he expected to get into the city. For a Monday, the traffic was thick and slow. When he made it through the city and into the parking garage, it took time to find a parking spot. Ryan was getting frustrated. He wouldn't have a lot of time to prepare for lunch with Barry. He had hoped for more time.

In the elevator, he texted Barry that he had arrived and would meet him shortly. Madison still hadn't answered his text. He couldn't resist the urge and sent her another one.

If I can help with anything let me know.

He closed his phone, stepped off the elevator and headed towards his office. He felt his phone buzz. Pausing in the doorway of his office he checked his messages.

Did you really leave? You didn't say goodbye.

Ryan closed his eyes. He felt the air rush out or him while his shoulders sunk. How could he have forgotten to message Jake. They had gotten closer over this vacation. There was no excuse for leaving without saying goodbye.

I'm sorry Jake. I should have texted. Let's get together again soon. Okay?

OK was all that Jake replied.

Ryan was not doing well with his personal relationships. There was nothing he could do about it at that moment. He docked his laptop and turned it on. He checked his emails for any last-minute problems, but nothing new had come up.

No one was in the board room when Ryan arrived. He did not like to be the first person to sit. Instead, he stood by the wall of windows looking out over the city. Gray clouds had settled low in the sky. The glass and steel of the buildings around them seemed dark and foreboding. The river below looked cold. The door opened behind him, and Ryan turned to see who had arrived.

The last time he had seen Barry was a month ago when he had given his notice. The man who stood before him barely resembled the man he had been. He had lost weight and his hair had thinned to a fuzz. Instead of a sharp suit jacket, he had on a thick sweater. Barry's appearance shocked Ryan, but he didn't react. There was plenty of time to find out what was going on and why Barry had been so insistent on meeting with him.

"Have a seat. It will be the two of us today." Barry sounded hoarse, which was so unlike his usual vibrant voice. It disturbed Ryan and he eyed Barry coolly. Something was very wrong with his boss.

Ryan took a seat next to the head of the table. Barry took the seat across from him and smiled. Barry's personal assistant brought in a tray with their meals. He served them and pulled the beverages they requested out of a small fridge tucked away in the corner. He left them to eat alone, closing the door behind him.

"Thanks for joining me for lunch. I don't have the energy to go over to Sylvester's today. On days like today I take my lunch in here. I do love the view."

"It's no problem at all." Ryan opened his lunch container.

"I hope you don't mind the salmon. I would have ordered us the steak, but I can't seem to stomach it lately. I'm not sure why, but I still crave a good salmon."

"It smells delicious. I'm sure it's excellent." Ryan waited for Barry to explain why they were there, but he quit talking and started eating.

"Eat while it's still warm." He motioned towards Ryan's plate. "You can't beat the salmon dinner from Sylvester's."

Ryan could, in fact, but right now he needed to focus. Pushing Madison and the Sunflower Café out of his mind as best he could, he tried to enjoy the meal in front of him. He didn't want to be rude, but he wished he could be anywhere else than at that table.

"How was your trip?" Barry asked.

"I enjoyed the time with my family. I haven't seen some of them in a long time. It was great spending time with my brother, too. We don't get enough time together."

"Very nice. We need to make time for what's important to us."

"I agree." Ryan's mind raced. What was going on here? Lunch and small talk? What was the crisis?

Barry looked terrible. Ryan hoped he was all right but didn't feel comfortable asking about it. Instead, they stuck to small talk through the rest of the meal. Barry placed his napkin over his plate when he finished eating, but Ryan knew he only managed a third of his food.

Standing slowly, Barry smiled at Ryan. "It's quite the view from here." He walked over to the windows and looked out over the city.

Ryan stood next to Barry. "It's a spectacular view."

Even with the river below, the scenery consisted mainly of skyline. The differences between the buildings surrounding him and the open spaces at the lake weren't lost on Ryan. He already missed the green of the trees and the golden fields of wheat around the crystal blue waters of the lake. The next five days would be a struggle. He had to get back to the lake and to Madison.

"I apologize for strong arming your return, but there are some things you should know." Barry took a seat at the table. Ryan sat next to him and leaned back in his char. He might as well get comfortable with this conversation. He had a feeling it wouldn't be a pleasant one.

"First of all, no one knows you gave your notice."

Ryan inwardly flinched but kept his face passive. "Why is that?"

"Because I'm dying. I'm riddled with cancer. It's not responding to the chemo."

"I didn't know. I'm so sorry. Is there anything I can do?"

"I appreciate the sentiment, but no. There is nothing anyone can do."

Ryan nodded.

"I've told the board I won't be here much longer. To be frank, when they brought up my replacement, there weren't many names mentioned. However, yours seems to be at the top of everyone's list."

"I see." Ryan hoped Barry couldn't see the turmoil inside.

"There's an opportunity for you here. I thought you should know."

"I don't know what to say. I had no idea you were ill. It's a surprise that the board thinks so highly of me. I'm flattered."

"You've got the right background, an excellent education and phenomenal track record here. It shouldn't be surprising. The board will meet tonight to consider next steps. If possible, they want to hire my replacement before I have to step down. This process needs to move fairly quickly to ensure a seamless transition. Think it over."

"It's a lot to think about. I had intended to move in a different direction."

"It's a complicated situation. I had hoped to tell you sooner, but I didn't know where we stood when you gave your notice." Barry gave an inconsequential shrug.

Ryan hesitated before responding, "So, you kept it quiet."

"It's still valid. You've fulfilled the terms of your contract. If you walk away, you walk away with your severance."

Ryan leaned back in his chair. "Good to know."

Barry stood up. "Thank you for joining me for lunch today."

"Thank you for having me." Ryan stood as well and shook Barry's hand.

"All of this is under wraps. Privacy will be maintained no matter what you decide." Barry walked Ryan to the door.

"Very good. I'll give it some thought." Ryan went back to his office and sank into his chair. He pulled out his phone to call Madison. It rang through to her voicemail.

"Hi, it's Ryan. How are you doing? Give me a call."

He stared at his phone. Madison must be busy. She had so much to take care of. He should be there for her. He wanted to tell her about his lunch and the decisions he needed to think through. There was a lot to talk about.

This put a whole different spin on everything. What if he took his time with the farmland? He could hire someone to get it planted and manage it. The house could be finished before he moved out there. He could stay in the cities and visit Cloud Lake on weekends and vacation days. Depending on the compensation package, he could put in another five or ten years at the company. He would still live out his dream, but he would have to do it from a distance at first.

Ryan put his thoughts aside and tried to concentrate on work. His head wasn't in the game. He put a few hours in but didn't accomplish much of anything. Finally, he gave it up and left for home.

The silence of his house disturbed him. The sea of boxes was a stern reminder this wasn't home anymore. In a few short weeks, the house would belong to somebody else.

He set his briefcase next to the hall table. Everything on it had been packed away, including the tray he used to put his keys in. He had brought his suitcase in and took it to the bedroom to unpack it. His room was bare besides the essential furniture. The kitchen was empty as well. He would have to order in for supper.

It was a stark contrast to the past few days with Madison. Her small cabin was simple, but full of life and love. From the quilt on her bed to her refrigerator full of fruit, her cabin seemed more like a home than his house ever had.

She still hadn't responded to his messages. Ryan tried texting again.

I'm sorry I had to leave. I've been thinking about you all day. Are you all right? I'm here if you want to talk.

CHAPTER 25

*E*xhaustion overwhelmed Madison. It had been a full day of phone calls. Afterwards, she had supper with her grandparents. She enjoyed their company but had left soon after they were done eating. She needed the comfort and security of her own home. All she wanted was to put on her pajamas and crawl under the covers of her bed.

When she entered the cabin, she didn't bother turning on the light. Instead, she turned on the lamp on her nightstand. She found a soft set of pajamas and got ready for bed. Her phone buzzed with Ryan's message. She considered calling him, but she was so tired. She lay in her bed, pulled her quilt up to her chin and fell asleep.

Madison slept fitfully but stayed in bed until almost noon. She considered staying in bed all day, but her stomach growled. She started the coffeemaker and stared at fridge. It was full of food, but she couldn't decide what to eat. Eventually she decided on a fried egg sandwich and hash browns. She pulled out a container of blueberries to snack on while she cooked. It didn't take her long to shred a potato and fry everything up.

She took everything over to her table, grabbed her phone off the nightstand and sat down to eat. Madison took a sip of her steaming hot coffee and scrolled through her phone. She had turned off all of the notifications. Calls and texts flowed in constantly and it was distracting. Most of the messages were people sending their sympathies. She didn't return those – there were too many of them. Chloe had left five messages. Those she would answer after she finished eating. There was a voicemail from a number she didn't recognize. She listened to that one first.

The fire department liaison had left the message. They had cleared the building for her to go in. The official report would take time, but the cause of the fire seemed to be a lightning strike overloading the electrical system. They would provide more information when the report came out. Relief washed over Madison. The fire was an accident. No one could have prevented it from happening.

Madison messaged Dylan, telling him she received the all-clear to enter the building and asking when he had time to meet. He responded right away, saying he would be free in an hour and could meet her there. She messaged Chloe the news and Chloe messaged back she would pick her up. They could meet with Dylan together.

She needed to answer Ryan. She knew she wasn't treating him fairly, but she couldn't bring herself to message him. Madison decided to get ready first. After doing the dishes, taking a shower, and getting dressed, she felt ready to text him.

Staring at her phone, she felt her chest tighten. Trying to find the right words was harder than she imagined it would be. She wanted to tell him off for leaving her to face everything alone, but she also wanted to tell him how much she missed him. There were too many feelings tumbling around inside of her. It made her heart ache. She decided to keep things simple.

I'm fine. How are you? Heading to the café soon. Busy day again.

He responded right away.

I'm fine too. Can we talk later?

Madison didn't want to but knew she should.

Sure. I'll be home this evening.

She could sense a headache coming on. She rubbed her temples and tried to relax. It would just be a phone call. With all she had been through the past few days, she could handle it. Madison could handle anything.

Chloe honked her horn when she pulled into the driveway. Madison grabbed her travel mug of coffee. Exhausted, she hoped the caffeine would help perk her up.

"What in the world are you wearing?" Madison asked as she climbed into the Jeep.

Chloe wore navy blue cropped dress pants and a light green mock turtleneck tank. She wore a long necklace made out of navy stones that matched her wedge shoes. Madison scrutinized her own outfit of ragged cut-off shorts, faded old tank top and the tennis shoes she usually used in the garden.

"Did I miss a memo somewhere? Is there a dress code for checking out burned down buildings?" Madison teased Chloe.

Chloe grinned. "It's my new look. I'm going for business chic."

"It looks great! I was going to say you could have warned me, but I think I still would have worn what I'm wearing."

"I tried to warn you, but you weren't answering your phone!"

"I have the ringer off. I'm still getting so many phone calls. That and I slept until noon." Madison was grateful Chloe let the last comment pass.

"Actually, I had an interview this morning and haven't had a chance to change."

"That sounds so weird. It's good though. Where was it at?" Madison asked, curious about Chloe's choice of outfits.

"The bank has a temporary opening. One of the tellers is taking twelve weeks of maternity leave." Chloe looked over at Madison. "It does sound weird, doesn't it?"

Madison nodded.

Dylan was already at the café when they pulled in. He was leaning against his truck with an arm resting on the tailgate and his other hand tucked into his jeans pocket.

"Damn, Dylan. If you weren't married, I'd use my birthday candles to wish for you."

"Chloe!" Madison couldn't believe her friend some days.

Dylan laughed. "Darlin', you're too hot for me. I'd end up worse than this café. Burned to ashes. Look at you all dressed up."

"I clean up nice, don't I?" Chloe struck a pose.

"You're going to get awfully dirty if you're coming in with us," Dylan told her.

Chloe shrugged. "They're just clothes."

"Do you want this?" He pulled a flannel shirt out of the truck and offered it to her.

"Thanks, this should help." Chloe put it on and rolled up the sleeves.

"Are you ready?" he asked Madison.

"I hate this," she said. Tears prickled her eyes. Her hand clenched so tight that her nails dug into her palms.

Chloe linked her arm through Madison's. "We do too. Let's go."

Madison knew it was bad, but that didn't prepare her as she stepped into the building. If it wasn't black from the fire, it was soaked and water damaged. Everything from the red gingham curtains to the swivel stools at the counter were ruined.

Dylan didn't waste any time and began to work, taking notes in a small pocket notebook. Quickly and thoroughly, he went through the restaurant. Chloe followed him around, helping him measure and pointing out problems. Madison wandered through in a daze. The dining room was ruined. The wait station was ruined. The kitchen was ruined. She stepped into her office. The safe was still intact.

Madison went out to the Jeep and rummaged through the glove compartment. She didn't find what she was looking for and rifled through the center console. Under the receipts and napkins, she found a wad of grocery bags. Taking a couple, she went back to the office to open the safe. Unsure of what to expect, her hands shook as she turned the old metal dial. It took her three tries to get the heavy metal door to creak open.

Everything inside looked fine. Nothing was burned or soaked through. She pulled out a small stack of papers and the cash deposit bags that still needed to go to the bank. She emptied the cash float. That needed to get deposited as well.

The computer had melted into a pile of plastic. Madison could upgrade to that laptop now. Everything was saved to the cloud, so those files were safe. Everything in the filing cabinets was ruined. They were a burned and soggy mess. A lot of paperwork would have to be replaced. The thought of redoing all of it rattled Madison's nerves.

She left the ruined office and searched for Dylan and Chloe. She found them in the kitchen.

Clearing her throat, she caught their attention. "I need to run to the bank. How much longer do you need here?"

"I shouldn't be too much longer. You don't happen to have any blueprints of the place, do you?"

Madison dug into a grocery bag. "The building is old, so there isn't much to them. They look like sketches to me." She pulled out a file of yellowed papers.

"Where did you find those?" Chloe asked.

"The safe survived. They were tucked away in the bottom along with some insurance policies and old menus."

Dylan studied the drawings. "I could use these. Do you think you could sweet-talk a teller at the bank into making copies?"

"I can try. Chloe, are you coming with, or can I take your keys?"

"Take the Jeep. I'll stay and help Dylan."

Madison was happy to get away from the café. The sight of it horrified her and the smell was even worse. Chloe had left the top of the Jeep off. The fresh air whipped around Madison as she drove away. It felt cleansing. She cranked up the radio, trying to drown out the dark feelings and aching heart.

At the bank, Madison double-checked the deposits and filled out a slip for the float money. The teller agreed to make Madison copies of the café plans. She gave Madison folders, one to hold the originals and one to give Dylan.

Madison didn't want to go back to the café right away. She went to the gas station to buy a soda and a box of chocolate-covered raisins. She took the long way around the lake. The music was as loud as it could go. She ate her candy as she drove and tried to concentrate on the sweet raisins and bitter chocolate. The wind whipped her hair until it was wild. She tried as hard as she could to shake off her gloom, but it wouldn't budge.

Dylan and Chloe were waiting outside of the café for her. She handed Dylan the folder with the copies of the restaurant plans.

"This is great. Thanks, Madison. Tomorrow, I'm going to get this place boarded up, so no one messes with what's left of it. I'll start putting everything together for the permits you're going to need. Once I get these plans updated, I'll have you review them before we get to work."

"No thanks." Madison gave Chloe a look like she was sizing her up. "Are you ready to take over?"

"The restaurant? Sure, when it's rebuilt. I'll be here with bells on."

"How about now?"

"What are you talking about?" Chloe narrowed her eyes at Madison.

"It's time for me to move on from the café. I never wanted it in the first place, and I don't want to be the one to rebuild it. If you want to run it, it's yours. Otherwise, I'm going to have it razed and sell the land."

"No way. Don't do that. Are you serious?"

Madison didn't hesitate, "I'm serious."

Chloe considered what Madison said. "I'm ready. I'll take care of the place, Madison. We'll get it rebuilt. I'll do an excellent job."

"I know you will." Madison smiled warmly at Chloe.

Dylan had been standing to the side, studying his feet. He scuffed his boot back and forth in the gravel. He gave a nod. "All right. Chloe, I'll be in touch. If you have any questions, give me a call."

Back at the cabin Madison wanted to make herself dinner and get back into bed, but Chloe wouldn't leave her alone. She didn't mention the restaurant. It wouldn't have done any good if she had – Madison was done discussing it for the day. All she wanted was some quiet to think through everything. She needed a next step.

Madison decided she needed comfort food. She made homemade macaroni and cheese, fried chicken cutlets, and to keep them healthy, served it with a side of creamed peas. Root beer floats with maraschino cherries on top rounded out their dinners. Chloe found an old movie for them to watch. Madison was relieved it wasn't a romance.

When the movie finished, Chloe offered to spend the night. Madison asked her to stay another time and shooed Chloe out. Madison told herself she wanted privacy to talk with Ryan, but after Chloe left, she didn't have the energy. Instead, she sent him a text.

Long day, too tired to talk

Madison washed, dried, and put away all of the dishes before she heard her phone buzz with his reply.

Get some rest. I hope we can talk soon. Goodnight, beautiful.

Madison didn't feel beautiful. She felt like the restaurant, a shell of what she had been. She crawled under her covers and cried herself to sleep.

CHAPTER 26

Ryan waited to see if Madison would answer him, even though he knew she wouldn't. He sat in a chair he didn't want anymore, in a house he only owned for another few weeks, in a city he didn't want to be in. He needed to do better. It didn't matter what people expected from him. He needed to follow his heart.

He texted his brother.

I need your help

He didn't have to wait for Jake to reply.

Sure bro. What's up?

Ryan called Jake and laid out his plan. The conversation didn't take long, and Jake was soon on board. Ryan turned out the lights and went into his bedroom. He needed to get some sleep. The next day would be a long day, and he had to be ready for it.

He slept fitfully until daybreak. After he woke, there was no stopping him. He rolled out of bed and put on his running clothes. Cool morning air greeted him when he opened the door to leave. Briskly, he walked through the neighborhood to warm up. The houses that surrounded his were big and beautiful with perfect lawns. He would not miss them.

He entered the walking path and started a light jog. Lawn sprinklers turned on, a dog barked from behind a fence, and he heard a siren in the distance. A car alarm went off and Ryan grinned. He wouldn't miss the city noises either.

Ryan broke into a faster run, pounding the cement until he could barely breathe. Unable to take another step, he stopped to catch his breath. He leaned over with his hands on his knees and waited for the stitch in his side to subside. He caught his breath and turned around to walk home.

Next on his list was a quick shower and some breakfast. There was a diner close to a strip mall that he had in mind. It wouldn't be as good as the Sunflower Café, but it was good enough. There was a thick crowd when he got there. A young girl at the counter told him it would take twenty minutes to get a table. While he waited, he chatted with the people sitting next to him on a bench in the lobby.

When it was his turn to be seated, the host offered him a small window booth. The sun shone through the window with a warm light. The waitress stopped at his table and took his order of coffee and an omelet with ham and cheese. When she asked if he wanted anything else, he nodded and added a side of fruit.

The server brought out his coffee right away. Steam rose from the mug. He couldn't resist and took his first sip. Hot and strong, it tasted like heaven.

Ryan took out his phone to text Barry.

I appreciate what you tried to do for me. Unfortunately, I do have to leave for an urgent matter. I'll be unable to fulfill the last few days of my notice. I understand the consequences. Thank you for everything.

He drank his coffee and watched the traffic driving by the diner. Ryan marveled at how many cars passed by on the busy street. Never-ending streams of them could go by all day every day. The server brought Ryan his food and asked if he needed anything else. He shook his head and thanked the waitress.

Digging into his food he wondered how long it would take to get the Sunflower café up and running again. He hadn't realized it, but Dylan owned the company he hired to renovate his farmhouse. Dylan and his crew had been scheduled to start work, but Dylan asked if he could take care of Madison first. Ryan didn't need any convincing. He would have to stay at the resort longer than he originally planned, but it was well worth it.

He finished eating and settled his bill. He left the diner and walked over to the strip mall. It held a fairly large department store. He found his way to the men's department and started shopping. T-shirts, tank tops, jean shorts, and sandals made a mountain in his cart as he pulled them off of racks and shelves. He left with his arms full of bags and had to drop them off in his Escalade before his next stop.

The whole reason for his trip stood at the other end of the strip mall. A simple sign above its door read "Garneau's Fine Jewelry." He entered the small but elegant shop.

"Can I help you find anything?" The sales consultant greeted Ryan warmly.

"I don't know what I'm looking for," Ryan replied.

The salesperson gave him space to shop around. He avoided the engagement rings. Ryan had no plans of getting engaged any time soon. He wanted something special. He wandered the cases, studying the contents closely and considering the pieces. The birthstone rings were beautiful, but not quite right. One counter held a nice display of tennis bracelets, but that wasn't right either.

On the farthest wall was a display case labeled Summer Lovin'. The jewelry and gems it contained were designed with summer themes. Sapphires adorned small silver sailboat necklaces. Bracelets made for charms were surrounded by bright summer items: strawberries, suns, beach balls, and even a tiny hamburger. Rings had gemstones arranged into rainbows. But the edge of the case caught Ryan's attention.

The section was full of gems set into the shapes of various flowers. There were rose shaped pins and rings that looked like daisies, but what caught Ryan's eye was a necklace. A sparkling sunflower embellished with a small yellow diamond encircled with topaz gems in a variety of yellows hung from a delicate silver chain.

"Do you see something you like?" The salesperson appeared at Ryan's side.

"Yes. I'll take the sunflower necklace. It's perfect."

"Yes sir, it's a beautiful piece."

The salesperson rang him up, and Ryan was on his way again. This time, he drove to the airport. He parked in short-term parking and made his way inside. He ordered a coffee and found a chair to wait in. An hour passed before he spotted Jake. Ryan walked over to greet him.

Jake embraced him with a warm hug. "All right, bro, let's do this."

They put on their sunglasses and walked out into the sunshine.

"What's all this?" Jake had to push bags out of the way to make room for his backpack in the SUV.

"New clothes." Ryan grinned. "I even found a Feather Dreams T-shirt."

"Right on." Jake pulled up their playlist and they listened to them until their next stop. It didn't take long to get there.

"Do you want to drive the Escalade or the moving truck?" Ryan asked.

"I am definitely driving the moving truck. Look at this beast. How big is it?"

"Twenty-six feet. They didn't have anything bigger," Ryan explained.

They went in to sign the contract and get the keys. It took Jake a moment to get his bearings in the truck, but they were soon on the road. Jake had never been to his house before, so Ryan led the way. He parked on the street in front of his house and watched as Jake parked the truck. He backed the thing straight into the driveway. Ryan was impressed. Jake hopped out of the truck, and they entered the house through the garage.

Jake whistled. "Nice place. You lived here by yourself?"

"I've never had a relationship last long enough to have anyone move in."

"That's kind of sad, bro."

I'm hoping things will change." Ryan grinned.

Jake grinned back at him. "Let's get started."

They spent the next five hours stacking furniture and boxes into the truck. They only took quick breaks to catch their breath and rehydrate. The work was grueling, but they had everything loaded except their backpacks and the mattresses they planned to sleep on.

"I'm dying. Or I'm dead. Am I dead?" Jake flopped on the floor, laying on his back and staring at the ceiling.

"I think you'll survive. I'm starving. Want to go out or order in?" Ryan asked.

"I'm not moving. Order in."

"Pizza, burgers, tacos, wings? What do you want?"

"All of it," Jake answered.

Ryan shrugged. He knew the perfect place, a little pizzeria that offered almost any kind of pizza a person could imagine. He called them and ordered a taco pizza, a bacon cheeseburger pizza and hot wings. That should cover supper. He grabbed a couple of beers out of the fridge and sat on the floor next to his brother. Jake managed to sit up to drink his beer.

"I know you have the winery covered, but are you worried about your plans with Madison?"

"We're getting straight to the point then? Yes, and no. I need to give it one more try. If it doesn't work out, I'll move on."

"She turned the Sunflower over to Chloe."

Ryan rubbed the back of his neck and took a drink before saying anything. This news worried him more than anything. "Have you heard how she is doing?"

"This is all from the gossip chain, but Chloe told Jesse, who told me, she is miserable. The fire seems to be the thing that broke her."

"I never should have left." Ryan fidgeted with the cap from his bottle of beer.

"You did what you had to do. You're not responsible for Madison."

"You're right." Ryan sighed heavily. "She would hate the thought of it."

"Maybe you two will work out and maybe you won't, but starting a relationship where one person is too dependent on the other is recipe for disaster."

Ryan chuckled. "How did you become so wise?"

"I'm a freaking genius, bro. Just wait until I'm ready to take over the world."

Ryan laughed harder. "How are you and Jesse?"

"We've been having a fun time. His gaming setup is impressive. He's smart, he's funny, he's gorgeous."

"But?" Ryan prodded.

"I don't know," Jake admitted. "I'm heading to grad school soon. He works at a gas station. We're sort of on different pages here."

"I see how it could be an issue."

"We'll see how it goes. I'm done sleeping on his couch, though. It's lumpy as hell. I'm going to stay out at the resort."

"You're sticking around?"

"I don't have a lot going on."

The doorbell rang. Ryan grabbed the stack of boxes from the delivery guy and swung through the kitchen for another couple of beers. He set everything down and looked thoughtfully at Jake.

"I'm glad you're staying. We should hang out more."

"Definitely."

They dug into the piping hot pizza as if they hadn't eaten in days. Ryan couldn't believe they had the entire house packed into the truck and ready to go. He owned way too much. They even packed the SUV and passenger seat full of boxes.

He wasn't even sure he wanted much of it anymore. After spending time in Madison's cozy cabin, he had learned to appreciate simple, comfortable furniture. He didn't have time to sell it, and leaving it behind wasn't an option. It would need to go into a storage unit near Cloud Lake until he had time to deal with it.

They ate half the pizza and all of the wings. They both drank another beer. The conversation dwindled into silence and Jake called it a night.

Ryan knew he should go to bed, too. They wanted to start out early in the morning, He tried to sleep, but Madison occupied his thoughts. He wanted to know how her day went, but he also knew she didn't want to talk. Sending her another text would just bother her. As if she read his mind, she texted him.

Thanks for helping me when the fire happened. I appreciate you being here for me.

He smiled. She was talking again. This was good.

You're welcome. I'm happy to hear from you. You've been quiet.

Ryan didn't want to ask her to talk again. He would see her soon enough.

Madison sent another text.

I needed time to think. It's going to be best if we don't see each other anymore. I'm thankful for your help, but I don't want to see you again.

This was not good.

I understand.

He didn't know what else to say. Emotions swirled in his chest, but he couldn't explain them over a text. Things needed to be cleared up in person. He was too tired to figure things out. He would sleep on his problems for now and reevaluate in the morning.

Even though he was exhausted, Ryan woke before his alarm went off. He ordered coffee for himself and his brother. He considered getting bagels but decided they could finish off the cold pizza instead. He dressed and packed his last few items before the coffee arrived.

The doorbell seemed to have woken Jake. He came down the stairs with his hair like a scarecrow. Ryan took the coffee from the delivery person who looked surprised at his brother's appearance. Shutting the door with a chuckle he offered one of the cups to Jake.

"Oh, coffee. Oh yes. Hand it over."

"Good morning to you, too. Are you ready to do this again?" Ryan asked.

"No way. I'm beat. I'm calling in reinforcements to help us. There's no way we can unload everything ourselves."

Ryan felt it, too. His body ached in places he didn't even think possible. "Good idea."

Jake pulled the pizza out of the fridge and helped himself to a slice. "We should hit the road."

They took the last of Ryan's things out to the truck. Ryan threw out their garbage and went back in for his backpack. He took one last look around. With or without Madison, it was time for a fresh start.

CHAPTER 27

Madison sat at the kitchen table with her Grandpa Don. Grandma Mabel was cooking a feast. She had made pancakes, eggs, bacon, and sausage. A big bowl of fruit salad sat on the table with another bowl of fresh whipped cream next to it. Grandpa Don snuck his spoon into the cream, added it to his coffee, and winked at Madison.

"Is someone joining us for breakfast, Grandma?" Madison asked.

"Good heavens, no. I'm in my housecoat. No one else is coming over."

"It seems to be a lot of food."

"Oh, don't bother about that. What we don't finish, we'll eat tomorrow."

Madison thought they would have leftovers for the week.

"Just about ready here." Mabel called out.

Madison stood on the pretense of filling her coffee cup. She did fill it and then set it on the table so she could help her grandmother. She took an overfilled platter of pancakes over to the table. Then she carried over the platters of eggs, bacon, and sausage over as well.

"Aren't you a dear? Let me grab the syrup and we can dig in." Grandma Mabel fussed around the cupboards before coming over and joining them to eat. "Now, you were telling us about Chloe and the restaurant."

"Chloe's taking care of everything. She'll work with Dylan on the plans. She's dealing with the insurance company. I still have to sign off on everything, but that's about it. Chloe said I don't have to worry about a thing."

"What if she gets the job at the bank?" Mabel asked.

Madison helped herself to a spoonful of fruit and a generous serving of the whipped cream. "Chloe says she will be fine. It's only part time and temporary at the bank. It will take months for the restaurant to be rebuilt. I'll still be paying her, but it won't be her full salary until the café is open. Besides, having a part time job will keep her out of Dylan's hair while he's trying to work."

"What are you going to do now?" Grandma Mabel realized she hadn't taken any food and spooned scrambled eggs onto her plate. She took a piece of bacon and bit into it.

"I have no idea. I've been so tied to the restaurant. I don't know what I want to do. I've been thinking about the event center, and I might look for the right piece of land to build it. Or maybe I'll turn the main house into a B&B. I'm going to take a little time and think about what I want to do."

"Good for you, beautiful girl." Her grandpa smiled at her with his toothy grin. "You'll figure out a plan."

"You know, grandpa, I think I will." Madison smiled back at him. Part of her was still feeling anxious about facing a different future, but it felt right.

She enjoyed breakfast with her grandparents. Her heart overflowed with love for them. She couldn't change the past and how busy she had been, but her priorities were shifting. From now on, her grandparents were at the top of the list. She promised them she would visit again soon, and she meant it. Her grandpa sent her off with a kiss on the cheek and her grandma sent her home with a big bag of leftovers.

Back at her cabin, she decided it was time. She found a few empty totes in the garage and headed into the main house. Going through her parents' items would take time, but currently she had all the time in the world. She decided to start with the hardest room first. She brought the totes into her parents' room. For a moment, she sat on their bed. She tried to sense her parents in the room with her, but she couldn't. It was only an empty room filled with furniture and clothes.

Carefully she went through their closet. Some of her parents' outfits sparked memories. Her father had kept the shirt from the summer cookout where her mom had gotten mad and squirted BBQ sauce all over him. Her mom had kept the summer dress she had worn at Madison's college graduation. When a memory came flooding back, Madison would hold the piece of clothing for moment. She took the time to remember the happy times and some sad times too. Then she would pack the item for donation, or, in the case of the BBQ shirt, she would toss it out. There were very few things she put aside to keep.

The process was slow. She worked late into the afternoon and had bins spread all over. She would have to deal with them tomorrow. Her stomach rumbled. It had been hours since she had breakfast with her grandparents.

She went back to her cabin. She needed a quick shower before she started cooking supper. Her ringer went off the second she walked through the door. Madison decided whoever it was could wait. She gathered fresh clothes, and the ringer went off again. She grabbed her phone and saw Chloe's number.

"How many times have you called me in a row?" Madison asked annoyed.

"I dunno. Maybe ten? You weren't answering!"

"I didn't have my phone on me. Is there an emergency or something?"

"Yes!"

"Okay?" Madison bit at her lip. Now what was happening.

"We'll be there in about fifteen minutes."

"What? Who's we?" Madison stared at her phone. Chloe had already disconnected.

"I should have let it ring," Madison muttered to the empty space around her.

She raced through her shower and dressed in record time. She was blow-drying her hair when she heard her front door open. Chloe must have let herself in.

"Who is this we?" she demanded, coming out of her bathroom.

"It's your favorite chef. At your service." Benny took a bow.

"Benny! It's so good to see you!" Madison hugged him tightly. "I'm sorry I haven't seen you since you were in the hospital."

"No worries. I know you've been busy."

Chloe came in with her arms full of grocery bags. "Here we go."

"What is all of that?" Madison asked her.

"I'm making chicken enchiladas and jalapeno poppers," Benny said with a wink.

"And I'm making margaritas," Chloe added, shaking a bottle of tequila.

"In my tiny kitchen? Good luck." Madison shook her head and laughed. "You guys are crazy."

"I'm a professional." Benny wiggled his eyebrows at her. "Hey, what's orange and sounds like a parrot?"

"Another parrot?" Madison asked.

"A carrot!" Benny grinned.

Madison and Chloe groaned.

Benny set up a small workstation at her table to get the food assembled. Chloe went into the kitchen and blended the margaritas. Madison tried to help, but they wouldn't let her. All she could do was sit and visit with them.

The first batch of enchiladas were quickly assembled and put into the oven. Benny pulled out the jalapeno peppers and went to work on them. Another batch of enchiladas would go in after both the first batch and the poppers came out. Benny had it down to a science.

The margaritas Chloe made were delicious. Madison sipped hers slowly, savoring the flavors and wary of how much tequila Chloe had used. The icy drink was just what she needed after the hot, sweaty afternoon she had spent in the house.

Benny put the poppers into the oven and set the timer. He started the second batch of enchiladas. He kept up with his jokes and his stories while he worked. Madison thought he looked happy and in his element. She was a little misty-eyed thinking of their mornings together at the café, but she refused to cry. This time with her friends would be a celebration. Benny started telling an off-color joke about one of his nurses when they heard a knock at the door.

"Did you call the joke police on me?" Benny asked, widening his eyes and trying to pull off an innocent look.

Madison laughed as she opened the door, until she saw Ryan standing there.

He peered over her shoulder. "Am I interrupting?"

"I thought you were in the cities. What are you doing here?" Madison's voice dripped with irritation.

Ryan cleared his throat and shifted on his feet. His calm, cool demeaner was gone. "I would like to talk to you. After that, I promise I will leave you alone. Please, can I have a few minutes of your time?"

Madison glanced at her friends. Chloe made a gesture like she was shooing her of the cabin. Benny wiggled his eyebrows at her. Madison rolled her eyes at them.

"Sure, is the front porch all right?"

Ryan nodded. They sat in the white wicker chairs on her porch. He handed her a stack of papers and a jewelry box.

"What's all this?" Madison couldn't hide her surprise.

"The jewelry box is my apology. I'm sorry I left like I did. It was a stupid mistake. I don't make them often, but this time I did and I'm sorry."

Madison opened the box and saw the sunflower necklace. "This is stunning, but it's too much. I can't accept this."

"It's yours. You can wear it, give it to Chloe, throw it into the lake, but it's yours. I'm truly sorry, Madison. I hope someday you can forgive me for being so thoughtless. Maybe someday we can be friends. There's a connection between us that I don't understand and it's an unfamiliar experience for me. I wish we could start over – go on normal dates and get to know each other more slowly. I wish a lot of things. I feel awful for hurting you like I did."

Madison set the jewelry box on the table between them. "And these?" She glanced at the thick packet of papers.

"It's a contract to buy the resort. The winery is going to take a lot of my focus over the next few years. It's going to take a lot of time and effort before I ever hope to see a profit off of it."

"I don't understand. Are you saying you want to sell me the resort?"

"Yes. The best I can do is hire people to help Andy and Molly at the resort. You have a vision for it, similar to what I have for the winery. You'll do a better job with it than I ever could. You could turn it into something special."

"I see." Madison wasn't sure of what to do. Her heart was torn. She had been so hurt when he left, but she also understood he had to leave. There was a part of her that wanted to throw herself into his arms and accept his apology, but she couldn't bring herself to do it.

"Madison." Ryan left her name hanging in the air. She couldn't meet his eyes and stared at his shoes instead.

"I'm going to go. I'll leave the contract with you to review. There is no hurry. I have to go." Ryan walked to his SUV and drove away.

Madison stayed in her chair, staring into the space he had occupied.

A few minutes later, Chloe popped her head out of the door. "You okay, boss?"

"I don't know."

"That's okay. You don't have to know. Come back in and have an enchilada while they're hot. You still have half your margarita left too."

The smell of the enchiladas drifted out to Madison and her stomach growled. She couldn't resist Benny's cooking and went back inside to join her friends. She set the papers and the jewelry box on her nightstand to keep them out of the way.

"What is that? Is that a jewelry box? Did he ask you to marry him?" Chloe never missed a thing.

Madison raised an eyebrow at Chloe. "Oh, it's an apology necklace and a contract to buy the resort."

Chloe jumped up and snatched the jewelry box. She opened it and her eyes grew wide. "Wow, look at the bling on this thing. It is gorgeous! Benny, look at this thing."

Benny studied it a moment and shrugged. "It's a sparkly sunflower. What's with the contract?"

"He said he'll be too busy with the winery. If I want to buy the resort, I can. He said I would do a better job with it than he can." Madison blushed.

"Now that is a gift." Benny said.

"I'd still have to buy it. I don't know how the loan would work. It would be less of a loan from the bank, but I don't know if the fire affects anything."

"Wow." Chloe's face grew serious. "And all he did was go back to work when he was supposed to. I wonder what you'll get for Christmas."

"Let's forget about it for now. Those enchiladas smell amazing and I'm starving."

"Not on my watch!" Benny jumped to his feet and dished out the food.

The mood was more subdued than it had been before, but Madison enjoyed her friends' company. Time with them and some tasty food was exactly what Madison needed to lift her spirits. They stayed late into the evening. When they finally left, Madison was exhausted from another long day. She was curious about the contract, but it would have to wait.

Madison slept better than she had in days. She woke before the sunrise, feeling refreshed and ready to face the day. She started the coffeemaker and got ready. The jewelry box on her nightstand caught her eye. She loved how sunflowers always turned their faces towards the sun. She took the necklace out and admired the sparkling gems. On impulse she put it on.

Filling two travel mugs with coffee, she took them with her and went out into the cool morning air. She started her truck and headed to the north side of the lake. When she reached the resort, she backed her truck into the access across the road. Sipping her steaming hot coffee, she watched and waited.

It didn't take long to spot a figure coming out of the green cabin. He swung his arms to warm them and walked towards the road. She saw him pause when he spotted her. He jogged over to her truck and opened the passenger door to climb in. She could see he was wary, but she also saw something more. He was tall, tan, and handsome. He was kind and caring. He was smart and driven. He was someone she could fancy.

"Madison?" His voice broke into her thoughts.

She gazed into those stunning steel-blue eyes. "I'm sorry too. I've behaved badly. I don't know if we can really start over, but I'd like to try."

"We will. We'll start over and have a brand-new day."

She held out her hand to him. "Hi! I'm Madison Johnson. I heard you were the new guy in town, and I was wondering if you would like to have coffee with me."

He took her hand and shook it. "Hi. I'm Ryan Davis. I'm pleased to meet you. I'd love to have a cup of coffee with you."

Madison handed him the extra travel mug. "Want to go watch the sunrise on the other side of the lake?"

"This sounds like a date to me," he teased her.

"It's only a date if you kiss me at the end," she assured him.

"Then this is definitely a date. Do I have to wait until the end to kiss you?"

AUTHOR NOTE

Thank You

Thank you for reading Summer Lovin' at Cloud Lake!

For news, information and future book releases, sign up for Annie Lynn's newsletter at

https://tenderholtcreative.com/almnewsletter/

ABOUT THE AUTHOR

Annie Lynn Marene is a writer from Fargo, North Dakota. Her light contemporary romances are full of fun characters, humor and heart. She lives with her husband and two dogs in a hundred-year-old house. Her days are filled with reading, baking, hiking and travel.

RACIN' HEARTS AT CLOUD LAKE

A new beginning. A jealous ex-girlfriend. And they're off to the races.

Ellie Sutton needs a fresh start. Taking the opportunity of a lifetime, she packs everything she owns in her car and heads to Cloud Lake. She's made a smooth escape, except around every turn is the handsome mechanic that makes her heart race.

Josh Dudek broke up with his girlfriend months ago, but when he shows an interest in newcomer Ellie, jealousy rears its ugly head. As the drama accelerates at the racetrack, Josh has to keep his cool, not only to win the race, but to win Ellie's heart.

Coming in 2022

CPSIA information can be obtained
at www.ICGtesting.com
Printed in the USA
BVHW040216200523
664487BV00001B/103